Len Holden is a retired university lecturer and has written several academic books and numerous articles. He lived in Bulgaria for two years between 1967 and 1969 teaching English for the British Council. His next novel will draw on this experience living under a communist regime. He has also taught in Indonesia, Malaysia and Singapore. He has worked with universities all over Europe, and Scandinavian universities in particular. In retirement, he has been occupied by writing fiction and local history.

To Roper who are
doing excellent Work.

Len Holden.

I would like to dedicate this book to Marion my wife and Chris, my son, who have been an enormous help and support in writing this book.

Len Holden

A Sea of Trouble

AUSTIN MACAULEY PUBLISHERS

LONDON * CAMBRIDGE * NEW YORK * SHARJAH

A CIP catalogue record for this title is available from the British Library.

ISBN 9781035884698 (Paperback)
ISBN 9781035884704 (ePub e-book)

www.austinmacauley.com

First Published 2024
Austin Macauley Publishers Ltd®
1 Canada Square
Canary Wharf
London
E14 5AA

I would like to thank my son, Chris Holden, who helped with the research and writing of this book and was largely responsible for chapter 5 on The Thames Barrier.

I would also like to thank Anthony Hammond, at the Environmental Agency who took the time and trouble to allow me to interview him and who made very helpful recommendations for further research. Also thanks to Fiona Harvey, Environment Editor, and George Monbiot of the Guardian, for their support and encouragement, and the many articles published by The Guardian on climate change and its effects.

Table of Contents

Chapter 1
Canvey Island, 1953

Harry Rattigan stared out of his rain-lashed window at the corpse of an elderly lady floating down his street. "The world is going to hell in a handcart," his father said with a tremor in his voice. "It's bloody awful." Her face was half turned up as she drifted by. Her eyes were staring to one side as if alarmed by what had happened to her.

"Turn away, son. It's not good for you to see things like that," said his father, but Harry was glued to the scene in ghastly fascination. "Come on." He pulled Harry gently to one side. He felt a slight tremble in his father's hand as he looked up into his eyes.

"Well, Stan, two days ago, the sun was shining and we hadn't a care in the world," his mother said clinging to her husband's arm.

Yeah, thought Harry, *and I was playing football with my mates on the road down there.*

Stan patted his wife's arm reassuringly. "It'll blow over, Rose. You'll see,"

Mud-coloured water surged past the lower windows of the terraced houses. Debris of all kinds could be seen bobbing away in the torrent—dustbin lids, buckets, bins, fallen tree branches, bushes, plants and other detritus. His father and mother gazed down from the refuge of their bedroom window, riveted to the scene of devastation. Harry hung behind shocked and fascinated. They had been fortunate. They lived in one of the houses in Canvey Island that had two storeys. Those who lived in bungalows and prefabs had not been so lucky. Harry could hear people calling out for help. Some were crying others were screaming in a state of petrified panic.

Down their street which had become a fast-flowing river, men in gum boots splashed about trying to recover people, both the living and the dead.

"Bring that boat over here, Charlie," one of the rescue team shouted. The row boat was tethered to the shore by stays but still bobbed unsteadily in the rushing water. "Right, get that boat hook and try to get hold of 'em as they drift by."

One of the men leaned over the side of the boat stretching the boat hook as far as he could. One slip and he would be washed away too. "Gotcha," he yelled as he hooked the belt of the old lady. With the help of the others, they gradually pulled her towards the boat and finally heaved the body over the side.

"Dead," one of the men said gloomily. "Can't do much for her now."

"'Cept a decent burial," Charlie said. They looked grim and tired.

They pulled the boat to the edge of the land and gently hauled the body out where other men took over and took the corpse. The men rested by the boat gathering themselves for the next task.

"It's the worst I've seen, Bert. Worse than the twenties and that weren't good," said Charlie pulling out a pack of cigarettes and offering them to Bert.

"A high surge in the North Sea they said on the news. That sea wall which was supposed to protect us. Gone. Gone just like that!" he said snapping his fingers.

"Yeah I saw it…or what was left of it. Washed away like a sand castle in the tide." While they smoked, they contemplated the view.

Water reached the roofs of bungalows. Trees were sticking out of the water as if in the middle of a river. The tops of hedges could just be made out as if they were a new kind of aquatic plant. Roads could not be identified. The flood had spread wide with houses and buildings surrounded by water as if in the middle of a lake. The gardens were completely covered and could not be seen. Vehicles of all kinds floated along or were half sticking out of the water. Lamp posts, road signs and other street poles protruded out of the water indicating roads to nowhere. Rowing boats plied up and down the drowned streets looking to rescue people and pets. They were often too late.

The men got back into the boat their few minutes rest over and continued their bleak work on the freezing January night.

"There's someone calling for help over there." They carefully guided the boat towards the shouts. Stan was hoarse with yelling. He saw the boat coming nearer. "Over here, over here," his voice nearly giving out. The boat finally reached the house bobbing below the bedroom window.

"You alright?" The boatman called.

Stan put his head out of the window, "Yeah, we're OK."

"Can you move down a floor so we can get you out?" The boatmen said. By this time, Harry had awoken from his doze.

His father was leaning out the window and said in a loud voice, "Yeah, we'll give it a go."

The dawn was just breaking which enabled them to see the situation more clearly. The electricity supply was one of the first things affected by the deluge, and they had spent the night in darkness. They moved slowly down the stairs and Harry exclaimed, "The water's gone down a bit, Dad."

"Yeah, that's good, son, but the difficult bit will be getting out. You don't mind getting wet?" He turned on the stairs looking up at Rose.

"You two stay here until I get that window open." He waded into the living room with water up to his waste. He finally made it to the window and with some difficulty opened it. "Water's bloody freezing," he mumbled to himself.

He opened the window and water rushed in but soon reached a level where it settled. The boat outside was nearly at their level and Stan clamoured out. The boatman secured the boat to the house and held out his hand and then Harry and his mother climbed out and were hauled into the swaying boat. When they were settled, Rose said, "Thank you, thank you," to the boatmen. Tears were running down her cheeks. The boat unsteadily made for the dry patch of land where they were able to get out.

"If you walk up to the village hall, you'll get a cup of tea and a warm-up and maybe some dry clothes." They thanked the boatmen and made their way to the village hall, clothes dripping and sticking to their cold bodies. "At least, we're alive," Stan said.

At the village hall, many people were queuing for tea poured from a large tea urn.

"I'll see if I can get us some dry clothes. While you get the teas," Rose said hurrying to the back of the hall.

A man came up to them and offered them a blanket which Harry gratefully put around his freezing body. Water dripped on the floor. A man joined them in the queue and said to Stan. "You alright, mate? You look like a drowned rat."

"I feel like one," said Stan.

"Yeah, at least you're alive; other poor buggers didn't make it. Drowned in their own living rooms or bedrooms. Too old to get out." The man sighed.

"Not only the old," someone said further back down the line. "There was a young couple. Just had a baby. Bought a new pram. As the water rose higher, they were pinning their hopes on an early rescue. Rescue never came. Water gushed into their bungalow; there was no hope for them. So they put their baby in the pram and pushed it into the streaming water."

"Oh my God, how awful!" exclaimed a woman. The rest of those in the tea line remained quiet listening to the man's story.

"The wonderful thing was that the baby was saved. Men in a boat saw the pram bobbing up and down and caught it. They were amazed to see a contented baby sleeping through the whole terrible event."

"What happened to the young couple?" A young woman said.

"Oh, they were later found in their front room lying dead in each other's arms. They stayed with one another until the end," the man's voice tailed off choking with emotion.

The young woman began to sob. This was a tragedy which stayed in Harry's mind until the day he died. He was ten years old.

When Rose returned, she held in her arms an array of clothes. Stan and Harry went to the toilets and stripped them of their wet things and returned in rather ill-fitting but dry clothes.

"I'm going out to help with the rescue," Stan said.

"Be careful," said Rose looking a little concerned.

Many of the men had already volunteered, and Stan felt duty-bound to do the same. The grownups made the best of it, their spirits reinforced by strong cups of sweet tea.

Harry whiled away the hours playing cards and talking to his mates as well as trying to comfort his mother.

When Stan returned later in the afternoon, he looked exhausted. He sat down and drained a mug of tea and said nothing. Harry and Rose joined the queue for food which had been set up at one end of the hall and brought a plate over to his father.

Two men sat by one talking in a loud voice that they could overhear clearly.

"It's not only people that need rescuing. What about the animals? There's nowhere to put them," said the loud-voiced man. He was wearing an old army overcoat and blue beret.

"I brought Benji, my dog, to the hall but they wouldn't allow me to have him with me. So I took a bus until I got to dry open countryside and released him to fend for himself. What else could I do?" He looked around the hall bereft of sorrow and guilt.

Bored by being cooped up indoors, the next day Harry decided to take a look at the reshaped outside world. He couldn't believe the carnage. From the higher vantage point overlooking Canvey, he viewed houses smashed to pulp with wood and plaster strewn about and water lapping at the edges. Jimmy Fisher a school friend came up beside him. "At least, there won't be school for a while. It's underwater!" he said joyfully. Harry agreed but was not so enthusiastic.

They looked down on cars making their way along flooded roads with policemen directing traffic. Sometimes the rescuers' cars needed rescuing. Canvey Island Secondary Modern School was deep in water up to the ground floor windows. Helpers directed the homeless to buses and other vehicles which would take them and their few possessions with them to dry areas which had buildings converted to large dormitories. Harry and his mate knew that there would be piles of clothing and shoes that had been collected for those who had lost their belongings. Nurses and orderlies tended to the refugees.

A stench began to rise from the flood as effluence disturbed by the overpowering water was flushed from sewers. Harry started to cough and slightly retch from the overpowering smell. "Phwoa, what a stink," Jimmy cried as he put his hand over his mouth and nose. Both boys turned and beat a hasty retreat from the smell of decaying sewage.

When Harry was dying from cancer some 50 years later, he began to recount the events of that night to his only son Mark. Throughout his adult life, he rarely talked of it. The trauma was too great. For months after, he had difficulty sleeping. He saw the drowned arms sticking out of the flood waters and heard the moans and cries of the dying. These were the unrescued, the damned, the now forgotten. But he remembered. He knew many of those victims. The men, women and children whose lives were tragically terminated long before their rightful time. Mark sat by his bedside and listened as Harry rasping and gasping from his infected lungs related the events of that night.

"You know fifty-eight people lost their lives, Mark. Fifty-eight! And over a thousand in Holland. Poor buggers." He slumped back into the pillows.

"A tragedy, Dad. A great tragedy."

"Yeah." All energy seemed to leave him once he had told his story.

Mark, transfixed, gazed at his father as he closed his eyes and lay rasping and gasping for air.

As a hard-bitten reporter, he thought he could handle most tragedies; you did that by distancing yourself from the events. But this happened to his dad. It was as though he were there himself in Canvey Island in 1953.

Chapter 2
London

Mark put his key into the front door of the Brixton Edwardian semi. *The family home*, he thought. *Maybe for not much longer*. He dropped his bags. He did not relish the thought of facing Julie. Things had been building for a while and this might be decision time, one way or another. Two young children ran to greet him.

"Daddy, you are back? Where have you been?" His little six-year-old daughter Emma said. She was closely followed by an older boy James, tall for ten years.

"Yeah, did you bring us any presents back, Dad?" James said.

"What a mercenary little blighter you are," said Mark smiling, grabbing them both and kissing them. "Where I have been, there were no presents just snow and cold, cold ice."

"Does Father Christmas live there?" Emma asked eagerly.

"No, you idiot, you mean Lapland," said James with a sneer.

"Hey, you two, don't start bickering, I've only just got through the door. Where's your mother?"

"In the kitchen," said Emma. "Can we finish watching our DVD?" Mark didn't reply he was preparing himself for a possible confrontation. The kids returned to their DVD taking the non-response as a yes.

Mark gingerly walked into the kitchen. Julie, his wife was seated at a kitchen table. She was auburn-haired and still relatively youthful-looking for her 35 years. He bent down and pecked her on the cheek. She drew away slightly. He stepped back a little surprised and hurt despite the fact that he knew something was brewing.

"Well, you're back then," Julie said in a neutral tone. A tone which Mark knew was suppressing anger and tipping the iceberg of a number of unresolved issues.

Mark's response changed from hurt to resentment. "Nice greeting," he said sarcastically.

"What do you expect a ticker tape welcome? A bunch of flowers? I've been stuck here with the kids for two weeks and looking after your mum while you're off on a junket."

"It wasn't a junket; it was a work assignment as well you know."

"Oh, a work assignment. Yet another work assignment," she said raising her voice. "I so wish I had a work assignment. Just one. Not the string of work commitments which keeps you away from us. Your bloody family." She was moving into her stride. These were well-rehearsed words that had been stewing in her head for some time and now they were streaming out of her.

Mark's resentment was building but he kept it under control. "Do you mind if I pour myself a cup of tea?" Mark said with a touch of sarcasm which he knew would rouse Julie to an angrier level.

"It's your house as well as mine," she said curtly.

He poured tea and milk into a large mug and thought to himself, *This is getting us nowhere. I need to cool the situation otherwise it'll just turn into an all-out row and disturb and frighten the kids.*

He sat down on the opposite side of the table. "Look, I understand how you feel."

"Do you?" She responded sharply.

"Well, I…" Julie interrupted him before he could continue.

"You get all the fun and I get the drudgery. Washing, cleaning cooking day after bloody day. While you're away on important business," she stressed the last two words in a highfalutin voice.

Mark could see that a calm discussion of the issues was not going to happen. Julie had a lot of unresolved resentment which had been building up inside her for some time.

"It's not fun. I wish it were. It's the job which keeps the payments on this bloody house and all the rest." His voice trailed off. He was already betraying his best intentions.

"Look, Mark. This can't go on. You have to say no to some of these assignments. You're always away. If this carries on, the kids won't even recognise you."

"That's a bit strong." He hesitated gathering his thoughts but he knew he was going to say the same thing he had said a dozen times before and Julie would respond in kind. But he said it anyway.

"You know we need the money. Life in London's not cheap." Julie sighed as if to say, 'Not this old chestnut again'. He ploughed on with his well-rehearsed rationale. "Somebody's got to bring home the bacon. What do you suggest?"

"Look, Mark I've said this time and time again—can't you compromise? Go on some overseas assignments and spend more time at home. With us! Your family!"

"I'm a bit anxious. If I say 'no', they might not offer me so many or, God forbid, any."

"Well, it's us or the trips. You'll have to choose."

"Don't you believe in the issues anymore? You used to be more zealous than me about climate change. About the planet under threat."

"When you have kids and commitments, your priorities change. Yeah, I still believe in it all but I can't let it trample all over us. We have to be reasonable. What do you want to do…save the planet or save our marriage?"

"It's not come to that?" Mark was shocked.

"We've discussed this issue time and time again and now it's crunch time. You'll have to make a choice."

"But you were the one who turned me on to all this environmental stuff. You who went on anti-nuclear demos and supported Green Peace and Friends of the Earth. Gave up time for fund raisers went to all the environmental conferences and gatherings and all the rest of it."

"As I have already said, Mark. When you're young and without responsibilities, you can do that stuff. Now it's different. Yes, I attend the occasional demo pushing the kids in a buggy and go to meetings when you're here to baby sit, but we don't do much together anymore. It's beginning to look like your priorities, your work is more important than your family."

"That's just not true, Julie. I have to do this work. What else can I do? It's all I know."

"If you loved me, the kids, you would do less. Be here more. That you don't, tell me we are not the most important things in your life." Tears began to trickle down Julie's face as she said this.

Mark looked devastated. "I do love you and the kids. There's no one else if that's what you think."

"I know there's no one else," Julie finally said. "Sometimes I wish there was then at least I could have something real to fight against. Ideas, politics, climate change how can I fight that?"

Mark looked down. He coughed nervously.

"Errum…I…I have something to tell you."

"Oh, there is someone else?"

"No, of course not. It's just…" he paused.

"I…I've been given another job by the *Guardian* and I have to go in three days. I'm really sorry." He looked down glumly like a chastised schoolboy.

Julie said nothing. Rancorous heat was building inside her while she absorbed the words.

"OK, it's your choice. You've made that plain. If you go don't bother coming back here."

She rose rapidly from her chair and left the kitchen slamming the door. Mark sunk his head in his hands.

Julie was a woman who exuded strength. A woman who did not easily change her mind once it was made up.

The kitchen door suddenly re-opened. It was Julie. "I've been to see your mother," she said bitterly.

"How…how was she?"

"Not good. That's another problem, you can't deal with while you're away. Another job for me."

"Sorry."

"Don't be bloody sorry do something about it before you piss off on your next junket."

"Not good? In what way?"

"She's anxious. Lonely. I think she's reaching that stage when she can no longer cope on her own. She's getting more confused."

"I'll have to give her a ring," Mark said knowing that this was the last thing he wanted to do.

"Yeah, I think you'd better do that. When I visited her last week, she said that we never come around or contact her even though I phone or visit nearly every other day," said Julie despondently.

"Maybe she just wants us to visit more and she is putting pressure on us," Mark suggested.

"I think it's more than that. She is definitely more confused. I think she's reached the point where she needs a more secure environment. Something like sheltered accommodation or even a nursing home."

"I'll have to go over there and see for myself."

"Neighbours have said that she often wanders out and gets lost."

"Oh no, that is really worrying. Do you think she's getting past the sheltered accommodation stage?" Mark said anxiously.

"Probably. I think she needs some kind of professional assessment."

They both looked out of the window savouring the grim prospect.

"I'll visit Mum today and see how she is."

"Before you do, you'd better make your mind up. Us or this next bloody junket." With that, Julie left the kitchen.

Chapter 3
Greenland

Perhaps this is how it will be—the unchecked forces of nature. The ruins of time played out against a backdrop of uncomprehending disaster. What was once held firm and solid are but broken particles unstitched and floating free. Those walls of stone—lifted and thrown down like papier mache theatre sets. Washed away like the tidal sand to create another world. What have we done?

Mark Rattigan stood in the snow contemplating the view. The smooth white terrain stretched to the horizon, and although cold, a bright sun revealed a sharp beautiful landscape. It was hard to believe that all this could be gone in 40 years or more and that the cap of ice nearly two miles thick would be melted into little ice streams and finally sea water.

He looked down at the instruments that Olga Jensen was showing him and began to register concern. "The ice is melting far more quickly than was previously thought to have been the case," said Olga. "We based previous calculations on a melt 50 to 100 years time but the latest data is not good."

Mark Rattigan was to produce a long piece about climate change and his first stop had been to visit the Danish-run East Greenland Ice Core Project known colloquially as ee-grip.

"The aim of the project is to drill through the ice core and gain an understanding of past climatic conditions," Olga said. "In essence, the ice cores brought up to be examined will reveal thousands of years of the history of the climate. Its hot periods and cold periods give us some idea where trends are heading next."

"And what do you think those trends are?" Mark asked.

Olga's brow furrowed. "If the ice sheet is melting faster than we think, then it could have far-reaching consequences. Seas will rise more rapidly and low-lying countries will be badly affected. Pacific Islands such as Kiribati, Tuvalu and the Solomon Islands among many others will disappear under water." She looked out across the snow whose blue glow intermingling with the shimmering white highlighted her greying fair hair. Although now 58 years old, she was still a striking-looking woman—a person who commanded respect without the need to raise her voice or parade her numerous academic credentials.

"I think we need to go down into the tunnels for more information as that's where the drills are operating and where most of the location office data is held," she said. They made their way down into the intricate network of tunnels located beneath the ice cap. Mark noted the walls and floors carved out of the snow which glittered like some enormous fairy cave. It was indeed a totally unique experience for him and his admiration for the confident woman conducting him through this icy nether world continued to increase.

They reached a set of rooms which were a combination of offices and rest and recreation rooms. She indicated to Mark to sit and he pulled up a chair. "Would you like some coffee to warm you up?" She asked.

"I'd love a cup," he said eagerly.

She brought two mugs over, which warmed their hands while they sipped. Olga said, "Of course, another important effect will be changes in weather patterns."

"What do you mean changes in weather patterns? More sunny days as the earth warms up."

Olga looked sharply at him then her face gradually transformed into a smile. "OK, the usual response and I only wish that would simply be the case." She continued, "The weather will change as it is now, but there will be more extreme weather events such as hurricanes and deluges of rain. These occurrences will not only affect low-lying islands but also the coasts and inland areas of large land masses such as Florida in the United States, Japan, and even Europe. The consequences could be far-reaching, even devastating. Bangladesh, for example, will be particularly prone. A quarter of its land already floods every year and with a population of 156 million the effects will be devastating."

"Not a happy thought," Mark said with typical British understatement.

Olga did not smile and Mark suddenly felt his remark trivial.

They sipped their coffee. "I'll give you a tour of the place," Olga suggested now smiling and relaxed.

"If it's not too much trouble? That would be good," Mark said conscious of his grovelling response.

"There's no point coming all this way without seeing the set up. Of course, some things we will be unable to show you," Olga said putting her mug down and rising from her chair.

"First the office," Olga said climbing some ladder stairs which led into a large pod. Mark was surprised but followed her up the stairs and entered a room with some tables with banks of computers and screens on them.

"Take a seat," said Olga pointing to a well-padded office chair. "By the way, this is Jan Ekland on secondment from Stockholm, Sweden." A tall, well-built red-headed bearded man rose out of his seat and shook Mark's hand.

"Good to meet you," he said in perfect English. "This is where we store our research data and other findings. It's like the engine room of the project."

"Jan, why don't you explain some of our findings to our British friend? I have to go and check the drill. When you are finished, bring Mark down to join me," Olga said.

"How can I help you?" Jan said.

"Olga explained that the melting ice cap would raise the level of the seas but she said that there would also be weather implications with devastating effects on low-lying countries."

"All that is true. As that ice melts, the seas warm up and cause a further disintegration of the ice caps and fields not only in Greenland but elsewhere. Our British and American fellow scientists have reported similar developments in the Arctic and Antarctic. The Swedish project to which I belong produced a study— 'The Arctic Resilience Report'. This was compiled by my colleagues at the Stockholm Environment Institute. When the seas warm, it has a knock-on effect. I believe that's the expression in English."

Jan turned to a large computer screen and said, "We have been carrying out monitoring and from the data we have accumulated, we have constructed various possible future scenarios of the effects of the ice melt. Firstly, the temperature will rise. From data also pulled in from the Stockholm scientists working in the Arctic, we know that temperatures in that area are about 20 degrees centigrade above what we would expect for this time of the year. It has been described as being 'off the charts!' Sea ice is at the lowest extent ever recorded."

On the screen was a chart showing a continual rise in the average temperature over the past 30 years, spiking sharply over the past five years.

"That seems rather worrying," Mark said for the first time showing enormous concern.

"Oh ya. It's been happening for a long time but has recently increased. More greenhouse gases have been pushed into the atmosphere. We are now recording vegetation growing in some ice regions."

"Well, isn't that a good thing? Food can be grown and water used."

Jan gave him a rather old-fashioned look. "OK, that's the thinking of someone who obviously doesn't know the region and polar regions in general. The one big thing ice does do is reflect sunlight back into the atmosphere and this keeps the planet from overheating. If you replace ice and snow with vegetation and dark seas the sunlight and heat are absorbed into the earth's surface which will heat up the planet and as this cycle increases year by year, there may be a time when there is no ice and snow in the polar regions. This means that temperatures will continue to rise which will have a devastating effect on weather patterns. Dry regions will get dryer and wet regions wetter. It will disrupt agriculture and probably cause mass migrations as people seek more moderate climates in which to live. This is an extreme scenario but it could well happen."

"Do the authorities know about this? Governments, international bodies?" Mark said becoming increasingly alarmed.

"We have published reports. Some newspapers report the findings like your own, but they only make the inner sections. It should be headlines!" Jan's voice rises a little.

"But what about government reactions?" Mark enquires.

Jan laughs cynically. "They pay lip service and do relatively little. Some politicians don't accept climate change is happening. Others acknowledge that it is happening but do not accept that it is due to human activity. Others attend the international conferences at Kyoto, Paris and Glasgow but really do very little to affect these developments."

Mark quickly took out a notepad and pen and began scribbling all this down. Some reporters used only recording devices but Mark still liked the old methods and ways of the journalist. It made him feel somehow more professional and more dignified in his job.

Jan continued, "The problem is most governments are in power for the short term and as most voters can't see what is happening then the issue is ignored for more seemingly pressing concerns. You can't see the effects of climate change on a day-to-day basis. So the issue gets, as you say, pushed under the carpet."

"What do you do with this information then?"

"We just carry on as long as the funding lasts. There are people in various government organisations that are supporting us and are trying to provoke some reaction, but it's an uphill task," Jan said.

"Thanks for the information this will make an excellent copy."

"Good luck with that," said Jan. "You'll need it."

"Ugh. Oh, yeah," said Mark. "I'd better get back to Olga. Do you know where I can find her?"

"She's probably by the drill. I'll take you there."

They both climbed down from the pod and Jan led Mark along an ice tunnel. Mark thought, "The last 15 years have been an interesting journey. Science graduate, school teacher and now environmental science journalist with a national newspaper. I would never have thought this would be a job I would be doing when I graduated wet behind the ears from Sheffield University and reluctantly went into teaching teenagers. It never really worked because I was unhappy and was striving for a challenge. An intellectual one." He had been lucky to make the transition at the age of 29 and was initially worried if he could make it in the competitive world of journalism. The change meant going from a general science teacher to gradually becoming a special correspondent in environmental science. This was not the most difficult part of the career change but the unusual hours and occasionally being away from his family, but he had grown to love the job with its challenges and he felt that he was doing something exciting but worthwhile.

"Here we are," Jan said jerking Mark out of his reverie.

The quarter of a mile or so of the tunnel had opened out into a huge cavern, where Olga stood with a group of men by a large rig.

Mark shook Jan's hand and walked over to Olga. She turned and smiled and beckoned him away from the rig so they could talk.

"I hope your chat with Jan was helpful," said Olga.

"Yes very," replied Mark.

"This is the main drill but instead of drilling for oil, we are drilling for ice. Tubes of ice to be more accurate. As we go lower and lower into the ice, the drill cuts a tube of ice," said Olga.

Mark watched the process for some minutes until Olga beckoned him down another ice tunnel which opened out into a huge storage unit. They entered the unit which had layer upon layer of ice cores all tagged and recorded.

"Each one of these cores," Olga said pointing at the carefully arranged ice tubes stacked on shelves, "represents a moment in time going back hundreds of thousands of years. Each ice core is different in that it indicates the kind of weather conditions prevalent in each era of time. Whether there were freezes or hotter moments, and everything in between."

"And we're entering a hotter period?" Mark asked.

"It looks very much like it. The science can never be exact. But we do know that the planet is warming up," Olga said.

"And that's caused by human activity such as burning coal and oil?" Mark asked.

"That's open to question and many climate deniers will seize on that doubt but the rising temperatures coincide very much with the industrialisation of the planet from 200 years ago. We are not making a political statement but stating a scientific probability."

"Thank you for your time, Olga, it has been very useful. Can I get back to you for any more information?" Mark asked.

"I'd love to see what you write. I'd check it for accuracy," Olga said with a twinkle in her eye.

"Of course," Mark said, "I wouldn't expect any less."

Chapter 4
Home Again, Naturally

There was a wrenching noise as the ice began to crack in a jagged line down through its enormous depths. Nobody heard this deafening noise. It was too remote, beyond the human ear and yet its impact was massive. Shelves of ice broke away. Fissures travelled down into the depths of its mass where runnels of ice streams became exposed. Gradually, large chunks of ice and snow fell towards the ocean. It was a huge break away from the mainland ice field of Greenland. The split created a rift and a floating free iceberg the size of a small country. The ice and snow began its long dissolution into the Arctic waters.

Mark pushed his key into the door. Put his bags down in the hall. Julie came out to meet him.

"I wouldn't put them down for long," Julie said in a steely voice.

"What's up?" Mark said.

"While you've been away, I have come to a conclusion. It wasn't easy but I have decided. Either you or me will have to go."

Mark had anticipated this scene. He had lived it over in his mind many times. *This was the final break then,* he thought.

"I won't bother staying. I'll stay over at my mother's then. Can I see the kids before I go?"

"They're staying at my sister's for a week so I can get a break."

Slowly, he picked up his bags. "Right then, I'll stay at my mother's."

Out on the street, he walked to a bus stop bound for the nearest tube station. He would have to change for Hammersmith. Although he had done this journey a dozen times before, he realised fully how difficult it must have been for Julie with two kids.

"Hi, Mum. How are you?" Mark said in a loudish voice as he entered the house and took his key out of the door.

"I'm in here," a croaky female voice replied. Mark entered the sitting room of the house where his mother and his father (when he was alive) had lived for much of their married lives. It had been cheap when they had bought it in the 1960s but now was worth a small fortune. A small fortune for Mark.

"There you are, Mum," he said craning over to hug and kiss her in the large winged chair. The room was boiling hot and an electric fire with all elements glowing blazed away near his mother's feet.

"How are you?"

Mark's mother Jean looked up at him from the chair. "I'm fine. Just fine. It's lovely to see you, darling. I'll make you a cup of tea."

"I can do that, Mum. You just relax," Mark said.

"I'm always relaxing. I need to do something or I'll go potty here." Jean got up unsteadily and walked into the kitchen. She filled and switched on an electric kettle and Mark sat down at the dining table.

"Where have you been, love? Julie said you had been off somewhere cold. Ice and snow."

"Yes, I have a commission to write a piece on climate change and its possible effects. I went to a research base in Greenland," Mark said not sure if she really understood what he was referring to.

Jean nodded and turned to make the tea. It seemed to Mark as if it had gone over her head. Mark coughed embarrassed and plunged in. "It seems you have been out on some jaunts."

"Jaunts? What do you mean?" Jean said.

"Well, the neighbours have found you wandering."

"Wandering? Oh no, I can look after myself," Jean said frowning.

"But they said you seemed lost and Julie had to come and help you," Mark said in an anxious tone.

"Don't worry about me, love. I'm alright. It was nothing," Jean said.

"But I do worry, Mother."

Jean poured the tea and took a biscuit tin out of the cupboard, opened it and offered it to Mark.

Mark selected a jammy dodger, "Thanks, Mum. I do worry about you." He hesitated before carrying on. "I…I think this place is too big for you now, Mum. You need somewhere more manageable."

"What do you mean? Too big?" Jean asked looking puzzled and hurt.

"Well, this place is far too large for you to clean and keep up," Mark said hesitatingly, but he had said it at last.

"I've always lived here and I shall die here," Jean said emphatically.

Mark sighed and thought, *It was going to be a hard job persuading her but it had to be done.*

"OK, Mum, but I want you to think about it. And no wandering off anymore."

Jean looked absent-mindedly at Mark, picked up her cup of tea and began to drink.

"You need at least a helper to look after the house."

There was a long pause. Neither said anything. Then Mark coughed self-consciously and finally said. "Mum, would it be OK if I move in for a small period of time?" He hesitated looking for a response.

She slowly looked up. "Mark, I'd love to have you stay but I can look after myself."

"It's more than looking after you," he said falteringly, his voice trailing off.

His mother gazed across the table, uncomprehending. Finally, the penny dropped. "Are there problems with Julie?"

"Er…um yeah. We're going through a difficult patch. She doesn't like me going away for work."

"I can understand that, Mark. You seem to be always away."

"Well, that's not quite true. Well, OK, I have been away a lot, especially this year, but Julie doesn't seem to realise that I have to do it to support the family."

His mother was silent then said, "Of course, you are welcome to stay, love, but you will eventually have to work out this problem together." Changing tack "I'll make up a room."

"Don't worry, Mother, I can easily do that," Mark said getting up from his chair. His mother rose to her feet as well.

"Let me do it, Mark love. I know where everything is."

A Quiet Drink down the Pub

Once his room was made up, he said to his mother he was going out for a drink and wouldn't be long.

Mark walked along the road worrying about what to do about his family and his mother. It had all come at the wrong time. He felt stressed and depressed. *I need this drink*, he thought and soon he found himself outside a pub, The Rose and Crown.

A drink might cheer me up, he thought, but he knew from experience that wasn't usually the case. Unlike the stereotype of the journalist 20 or 30 years ago, most did not do the 'Fleet Street run' anymore; partly because most newspapers had moved their offices away from the famous street, and partly because the drinking culture had changed considerably by the noughties.

He remembered his old editor, Jack Riley, a tough hard-drinking Irish man but a bloody good newspaperman. On most Fridays, the reporters, editors, sub-editors and some columnists who would make the journey into the city, especially for the end-of-week booze up, would join the throng as they left the office by 11 a.m. for various newspaper waterholes like The Cheshire Cheese. The older reporters scoffed that those pubs were for the tourists not 'real' newspapermen. The late morning drinks grew into an afternoon binge which would then progress on to the famous Wig and Pen Club, where Mark watched his old boss, now long dead, down a bottle of champagne, a bottle of red, followed by brandies. Then home on the commuter train at about 8 o'clock at night snoring past their missed destination.

Well, all that's changed now and probably for the better, thought Mark as he pushed open the door of the lounge bar. *At least, I won't die from sclerosis of the liver*.

At the bar was a man in his sixties who Mark immediately identified as a regular. He was dressed in an ageing tweed jacket and nylon trousers which had seen better days. "Hello, squire," he said to Mark. "Not a great day weather-wise." He was obviously seeking a bit of company. The few other people in the pub ignored him and a couple buried their heads in a newspaper.

Mark foolishly responded taking this as a social overture for friendliness rather than a lonely man's need for company.

"Well, the weather's been a lot worse where I have been."

"And where's that then, squire?" The bar bore enquired.

"Greenland," Mark said turning to the approaching barman. Mark ordered a pint of bitter and turned to sit down, but the regular began to engage him in conversation.

"Greenland. A bit chilly, eh? So what dragged you over there? It must be a bit bleak."

"Oh, I'm researching an article," Mark said vaguely trying not to get drawn into a conversation, walking to the nearest table and chair.

"An article for a paper or magazine or what? What's that to do with then?" The man said.

Mark knew that if he outlined the purpose of his visit, it could draw him into a long conversation or even worse, an argument. He could sense the pub bore was of the barrack room lawyer type to whom you could not argue coherently or sensibly. Unfortunately, he was proved right.

"You're not one of those tree huggers are you who want to save the planet for the polar bears?" The man scoffed trying to make it sound all jokey. Mark knew it was the voice of the true bigot. How could he get away? Mark upset by the encounter with Julie began to get angry. His annoyance with and his recent experience talking to his mother fused into an angry bubble. *Why should I let this arsehole get away with blatant prejudice?* He thought.

"As it happens, I have been studying climate change by looking at the research and findings of scientists working there," Mark said his voice slightly rising. At this stage, if Julie had been present, she would have calmed Mark or even urged him to finish his drink pronto and leave.

The pub bore picked up on the rising bile in Mark's voice and licked his lips. There was nothing he enjoyed more than a verbal tussle. "Can I sit down?" The man said ignoring the silent response from Mark. "So you believe in all this climate change nonsense then?"

"It's not nonsense, it's based on scientific evidence," said Mark huffily.

"Scientific evidence, eh? Look out the window, it's raining and cold and they say it might snow at the weekend. I can't call that global warming," he said grinning in triumph as though this observable fact was all the evidence he needed.

"You're basing that on one day or even one year of your own personal observation. These people have been observing changes for decades and they believe the average temperatures are rising so fast that it's melting the ice caps. That's going to have serious implications for the planet," Mark said pointedly.

"According to *The Daily Mail*, they have melted before," said the man pulling a newspaper from his pocket as though it were the climate denier's bible. "That means it's what they call it? Oh yeah—cyclical!" the man said in triumph.

Mark calmed slightly and reasoned that the best way to extricate himself from the situation was to appease the man a little.

"Yeah, there is something to be said for that argument. Weather and climate conditions have changed and are constantly changing. Long before humans had an impact on the planet, the Earth went through ice ages and periods of cold and heat. But now it's serious. It's happening so fast now. Climate research shows that this is truly unusual and out of character for those changes. It can only mean that human activity such as expended carbon dioxide from cars and other machines along with other forms of pollution has an immediate impact. Temperatures are rising much more rapidly," Mark said waggling his finger as he made each point.

The man was only half listening as he was too busy marshalling his own arguments to understand the true import of what Mark was saying.

"So it's down to cars, eh? I couldn't give my car up. I need it to get the wife to her hospital appointments and do the shopping."

"Well, I'm not asking you to give up your car just to take on board what could turn out to be quite a catastrophe," said Mark finishing his drink and rising from his chair.

"You off already?" The man said.

"Yeah, I have to get home to meet the kids from school."

"Oh, that's a pity. I was just warming to the subject. Get it? Warming!" said the man laughing heartily.

Mark smiled said goodbye and left. "That was a close one."

As predicted, his pint didn't really help him and the pub bore made things only worse. He slowly walked back to his mother's house.

Chapter 5
Thames Barrier

At the same time that Mark was leaving the pub, Gareth (Taffy) Edwards, yes his parents had been big Rugby fans, was cycling down the Thames footpath in Greenwich to start another night shift at the Thames Barrier Control Centre.

Gareth had worked the graveyard shift for just shy of 10 years. He'd never intended to remain in the job for this long, initially viewing his role within the Environment Agency as a stepping-stone into a career in meteorology and broadcasting. It made him cringe now when he recalled that his dream as a young man was to be a TV Weatherman.

After ten years in his current job, he was more realistic about where his career was heading and took pride in being a part of the organisation, tasked with protecting Central London from the risk of flooding.

Gareth's job was to monitor and collate data from around the United Kingdom, for sea level, atmospheric pressure, projected rainfall and tidal ranges. Banks of computer screens displayed the constantly updating data received from tidal gauges dotted around the coast of the UK, the Met Office, the Coast Guard and DEFRA. Gareth would then add this data into computer modelling software, which could predict the level of the Thames to within a couple of centimetres at any one time, or that was the theory at least.

When he started in the control centre in 2007, the equipment in the control centre was state of the art and the envy of similar flood prevention operations across Europe. Since then, a lack of investment, from successive governments, meant they were using technology that was now 10 years out of date. However, despite these obstacles, the Thames Barrier, to this day, has never been breached. How long this record would last was a constant topic of discussion amongst Gareth and his colleagues, being only too aware that the combination of government austerity policies and the increased threats from climate change was impacting the continuing effectiveness of the barrier.

The evidence available suggested that sea levels continued to rise and violent storms were becoming more frequent and there was now a consensus amongst organisations such as Greenpeace, Friends of the Earth, The Green Party, some London MPs and even a handful of executives within the Environment Agency itself, who were now of the opinion it was a case of when and not if the barrier would fail.

Gareth was, in all but name, the senior member of staff during the night shift, although procedurally, he was meant to defer to his operations manager, Derek Lassiter. Derek and Gareth had developed an interesting working relationship, where Gareth was happy to be in control of data analysis and liaise with the Met Office and other flood agencies across Europe, on the proviso that Lassiter left him to his own devices.

The night of 25 March had been fairly typical, Gareth had arrived at work 30 minutes early. The main purpose of his early arrival was primarily to spend time with Kath, his counterpart on the 3–11 p.m. shift (the control centre operated a daily 8-hour shift rotation system). Gareth had taken a shine to Kath since she'd joined the team six months ago and the feeling was mutual, although neither of them had built up the nerve to tell the other their feelings, although both were acutely aware of how the office gossips delighted in speculating about the content of their nightly chats.

Lassiter arrived at 11 p.m. on the dot and as usual, spent half an hour making himself look busy, while in reality doing very little. At 11.30, both men sat down for their nightly briefing. These briefings consisted of Gareth giving Derek the latest sea and river levels in the Thames estuary, tidal range and weather forecast and what the modelling software estimated the river levels to be for the next 24-hour period.

"Well, Taa-fff-ee me, old mucker," said Derek, emphasising every syllable, much to his own amusement, "what's that computer model of yours predicting for us tonight then, Armageddon?"

Lassiter didn't trust the modern technology and believed the first-hand knowledge of the river's ebbs and flows, that he had acquired working the Thames tug boats, which had serviced the now largely defunct East London docks, was much more reliable than some computer model. He maintained he could feel it in his bones when a storm was approaching and the stronger that sense the worse the storm.

"Yes, good evening, Skipper." (Gareth addressed Derek as Skipper as a way of acknowledging his past as a Tug Boat captain) "Nice to see you too."

Gareth often felt exasperated with Derek's cynicism, although he did have sympathy for him. The man had witnessed so much change over his 40 years working the Thames and when the docks had closed, he'd been forced to take a job he had no appetite for, with responsibilities he did not wish for.

He continued, "We're getting some very low-pressure readings in the North Atlantic, which has subsequently led to high surge readings at the Fulmar-A oil rig, east of Dundee. It's too early to accurately predict if they're going to cause us a problem in the southeast, we should know more by early morning. Chances are it will dissipate as these things usually do. Other than that, the projection for the next 24 hours is for slightly higher than average river levels for this time of year."

"OK, Taffy, keep an eye on it and let me know if things change. The last thing we need is another barrier closure this month. I'm already getting it in the neck from up above about this year's budget. Apparently, the increased number of closures is becoming 'financially unsustainable' whatever that bloody means! The directive from Environment Agency HQ is that we must not authorise any more closures unless the risk of an abnormally high tide in Central London is 'extremely likely'."

"Those bureaucrats in Whitehall are only concerned with balancing their budgets. How much do they think it will cost if we get it wrong just once and Central London floods? They'll have some flippin' 'financial sustainability' worries then." Derek made that annoying quotation mark sign with his fingers, to emphasise his last point.

"I know, Skipper, we have our bosses here at the barrier telling us to show extreme caution and close the barrier, even when the risk of a breach upstream is moderate while the Environment Agency bean counters are constantly banging on about budgets. The worst part is all these people are well aware that the projections we're working with can never be 100% accurate and there will always be some element of guesswork."

They both felt frustrated by what they considered to be ridiculous budgets and targets imposed by Environment Agency HQ in Whitehall. Between them, they had accrued over 50 years' experience in predicting the ebbs and flows of the river and their knowledge made them better placed than some pen-pusher in Whitehall to judge whether the barrier should remain open or closed.

"OK, Taffy, nightly rant over and done with, best keep an eye on that surge in the North Sea mind. I'll be in my office if you need me." With that, Lassiter got up and left the room full of monitors and whirring processors, an environment he'd never felt comfortable in. He went back to his office to begin his nightly ritual of Sudoku, late-night talk radio and studying the form for the next day's racing.

When Derek had left the control centre, Gareth thought he'd better just double-check the seriousness of the storm surge off the Scottish coast. He guessed that the best person to contact would be Kim Overmars, who worked on the Eastern Schlendt Barrier, designed to protect the lowlands of The Netherlands. The Dutch were even more cautious than the British about the threat from storm surges, understandably with large swathes of their country being below sea level. Kim and Gareth had developed a good professional relationship over the years and were always sharing information that their individual modelling systems threw up.

Gareth lifted the receiver on his office phone and called Kim.

"Hallo, Kim, gesproken, wie is deze alstublieft?" came the answer from the other end of the line.

"Er, hi, it's Gareth Edwards, at Thames Barrier in London, can I speak to Kim Overmars please?"

"I know it is you, Gareth," Kim replied chuckling to herself, "in case you were unaware, it is possible to get phones that display the identification of the person calling. When I saw it was you, I just thought I'd try to introduce you to a bit of Dutch, knowing how you English are always so eager to learn new languages!" teased Kim.

"Err firstly, I'm not English as you are well aware and secondly I already speak two languages Welsh and English. So I'm not so far behind you, Mrs multilingual." Gareth knew Kim was only teasing him, but was happy to play along with the joke.

"So, how is my favourite Welshman tonight, keeping your head above water?"

"All good here, thanks, Kim, I was just checking in with you about the sea levels recorded by the Fulmar-A rig this evening. How are things looking to you guys, have you got any sea level readings from further south in the North Sea?"

"Yes, we are aware of the high sea levels, but if they don't increase, the current level will remain comfortably below our barriers limits. What is worrying us more is the storm system moving across the Atlantic from the Caribbean. Our meteorological experts are saying that we need to monitor this system closely, as it has the potential to deteriorate into something much worse than what we're seeing at present."

"Mmmm, that doesn't sound great, Kim, our forecasters were aware of that system, but not as pessimistic about how it might develop. Do your people have an estimate as to when that system will reach the North Atlantic?"

"We're not too certain at the moment, but early estimates are it could be as soon as the beginning of next week. We will keep you updated with any changes in the situation and if you can do the same please?"

"Yes, of course, we will. OK, I'd better go and give my bosses an update, good to speak, Kim, I think!"

Kim hung up the phone and Gareth went to give Derek Lassiter this latest information from their European counterparts.

Chapter 6
The Houses of Parliament

Soon Mark reached the Thames and walked the river path eastwards. He stopped and looked over the embankment wall and gazed down into the muddy green placid waters. It was hard to conceive that this peaceful stretch of water carrying tourists on cruise ships and small vessels could be anything other than a benign London scene. Yet he was assured that a torrent caused by floods and a sea surge could transform that idyll into a raging deluge. He shuddered at the thought.

He soon came to the Houses of Parliament and made his way to the press and media entrance and spoke to the duty officer that he had an appointment with Sir Claude Trentholme MP, the well-known climate change sceptic. The security officer phoned Trentholme's office and he nodded put down the phone issued Mark with a pass and gave him directions to the terrace where they had arranged to meet.

After Mark was ushered onto the terrace, he began to admire the view of the river from this unusual perspective. He was soon jolted out of his reverie by a confident voice speaking his name, "Mark Rattigan? The gloom and doom man!" Mark turned and found himself face to face with a beaming Claude Trentholme, who held out his hand.

He was a large man bloated by too many good dinners and fine wines but he had the affable air of a bon vivant. "What's your tipple or are you dry when on duty?" He asked smiling. Although it was only 11:30 in the morning, he ordered a G and T for himself while Mark asked for a coffee.

"It was good of you to see me," said Mark.

"A pleasure, my boy. What can I do for you?"

"As you know I'm doing an article on climate change and I would like some balance so that all views are represented not just a diatribe on behalf of the Green Party and Green Peace."

Trentholme nodded approvingly. "Quite so, my boy. As you know I am of the other persuasion as it were. I think this global warming stuff is a load of claptrap and needs to be debunked," Trentholme said forcefully but with a slight hint of a smile. "I've looked into it and have been advised. Even had a meeting with David Bellamy another sceptic and well-known scientist. He gave me a lot of information. I've also visited the States as a guest of the Heartland Institute and I learned a lot from them as well."

"So what conclusions did you come to?" Mark asked gingerly.

"Well, the idea that a rise of 1.5 degrees centigrade is dangerous to the Earth's environmental balance is highly contestable. This is normal for the Earth and the rise of CO_2 gas is also challengeable. The heat increase is caused by water vapour which is not influenced by human activity at all."

"So you do believe that the Earth's temperature is rising? Fifteen years ago in an article in *The Telegraph,* you claimed that the Earth was getting colder not hotter."

"Well, one can change one's mind in the light of new information. Yes, I do now believe the Earth is getting warmer but I don't believe it is caused by human activity. It's water vapour, not CO_2. All this recycling stuff and avoiding carbon-based fuels will do nothing whatsoever to curb the rise in temperature. It's beyond our control," Trentholme emphasised this last point by tapping the table on each syllable.

Mark was surprised at Trentholme's knowledge even as a denier. *This isn't going to be a walkover*, Mark thought, He tentatively countered.

"But we are well on the way to having a temperature rise up to and beyond 2, possibly 3 degrees centigrade. Doesn't that alarm you? The ice caps are melting and the glaciers too."

"This is the natural climate cycle of the earth. It's happened before. There was a rise in temperature in the Middle Ages and a mini ice age in the seventeenth century. My God, the Thames froze over!" exclaimed Trentholme getting more excited. They both gazed at the placid dark green river flowing past the Commons terrace. Mark found it hard to imagine people on ice skates gliding by.

He was about to pose another question when Trentholme continued his rant, "All this rubbish about rising seas and islands going under the ocean. Well, I haven't heard of any widespread evacuations. Have you? It's all nonsense."

"The indigenous people in those communities are worried. They have witnessed a sea rise," Mark stated trying to present the neutral face of reason.

"Poppycock. We heard all this at Cop26 and most of those communities and island nations are still intact, apart from Tuvalu of course, which was rather unfortunate for these poor blighters. Although that is a one-off and when it happens more regularly, I'll believe it," Trentholme confidently stated. Before Mark could interject, Trentholme continued with his tirade, "All these climate change vegetarian, sandal-wearing beardies are just creating alarm and they turn in rage on their critics because they lack confidence in their case. I've witnessed the handwringing at these climate conferences as Peter Hitchens wrote in *The Daily Mail* 'It's a festival of panic and exaggerated woe'."

Mark finally got a word in, "But the vast majority of scientists and politicians now agree that the use of fossil fuels is dangerous to the human race and needs to be phased out, even if, as you say, it's not caused by climate change. Look at the pollution caused by coal and oil-based emissions in China and many large cities in the east. People are being poisoned."

"So how will we fuel our economies? Wind power can't do it. Solar power can't and neither can wave power. If we are to maintain our quality of life, then we have to continue using fossil fuels and nuclear energy. They are cheaper and more efficient. I know President Trump is of this view. There is no other way."

"So we have to sacrifice the lives of hundreds of thousands of people so the west can maintain its living standards?"

"That's a bit below the belt, old boy. I am sure the scientists and engineers can find a way to limit the polluted outpourings of these facilities. I am certain technology can solve these problems."

"I do hope you are right," Mark said.

Trentholme made a great play at looking at his watch. "Well, it's been a pleasure but I have to run now I have a committee meeting to attend." He rose from his seat and shook Mark by the hand. "Let me know when the article is published. I think I'll enjoy reading it. If, of course, you quote me accurately."

Mark nodded, smiled and bade him goodbye.

Chapter 7
A Friend in Need

Mark sat down with his pint of bitter and looked at his watch. Jake's late. *He's always late*, thought Mark, *what's new?* Jake was one of Mark's oldest friends. They had met at university and hit it off pretty much instantly. Mark, the thoughtful, hard-working swat and Jake, the happy-go-lucky, take-life-as-it-comes kind of guy.

They had both been on the history course at University College, London and both ended up teachers. Mark had taught history in a comprehensive school in north London but had never really been happy. The kids were alright, or most of them, but his discontent was more about purpose. What was his raison d'etre? He came to the conclusion it wasn't teaching. He had a longing to get away from the cooped-up environment of the classroom. He wanted to travel, take on big issues, and do something to change the world. The catalyst came one summer when he had taken a course on ecology as something different from teaching history. It had caught his imagination and it changed his life. He now felt he had a purpose.

Determined to change career path he'd taken a part-time degree course at the Open University in Environmental Science. He reckoned that it was one thing that had kept him sane.

He looked down into his beer and ruminated. "Hi, Flubs," a voice behind him said rather loudly causing him to jerk out of his reverie.

"Oh, Jake, you nearly made me spill my beer."

"That's the whole idea, Flubs," Jake grinned sitting down and patting him on the shoulder.

"Don't call me Flubs, you know it pisses me off."

"Ooo touchy, touchy," Jake said although he knew better than to continue with the stupid joke. "Want another one, mate?"

"Why not? I've nearly finished this one waiting for you."

Jake had taken to calling Mark Flubs after the wonder material featured in the film 'The Absent-Minded Professor'. 'Flubber', an amazing material invented by the professor gained energy every time it struck a hard surface. Shoes made from it could jump to incredible heights and it enabled a Model-T to fly. Mark had speculated with Jake and friends, one drunken night after seeing the film at college, that it would be great if fossil fuels could be replaced by Flubber. No more pollution, no more threats to the planet.

For some time after, Flubber shortened to Flubs had been Mark's nickname. When Mark started going out with Julie, Jake had used the 'F' word in front of her. Such was Mark's embarrassment he had torn Jake off a strip with a reddening face revealing a mixture of shame and stupidity. Julie had said that it didn't matter and that it was only a joke. She had even said, "It's kind of cute," in that awful American way.

Jake returned with a couple of pints and sat down beside Mark. "Well, how's things, *Mark*?" He said emphasising Mark's real name and taking a long drink from his pint.

Mark ignored the false attempt at placation and said, "Not so good. Julie's thrown me out and I'm living with my mother."

"Classic," Jake said still avoiding being serious-minded but embarrassed for Mark. Jake sobered his voice. "That's tough, what happened?"

"She thinks I go away too much leaving her to look after the family. It's all got to her."

"I can see her point, mate, and I don't mean that in a critical way. You do travel a lot."

Mark thought that even Jake was not on his side. He was truly alone. He sipped his beer and looked downcast.

Jake put his arm around Mark, "Come on, I'm a mate. You know I'll always be there for you. If you need a room or whatever."

"You don't understand. I can't explain." Tears began to well up in Mark's eyes.

Jake noticed his watery eyes and tried to head off feeling sorry for oneself blub. "Come on," he repeated. They sat in silence while Mark began to compose himself. He sighed.

"I love Julie and the kids but I have to…" Mark faltered.

"Save the world?" Jake said. "You've always been like that. You can't do it on your own."

"If only I can get the stuff out there, people will understand. Take action. The bloody politicians and businessmen either ignore the issues or treat it as a joke or worse, deny it's happening."

Realising he was going into misery mode again, Mark made an attempt to control himself. "You know the issues, Jake. We've been over them many times."

Though Jake was a joker, he acted that way to hide his sensitivities and empathy for people. You can get hurt by being too much of a friend. But his love for Mark was deep and he thought *better let the old bugger get it off his chest. It might help. I can suffer the repetition.*

"What's making you upset besides the marriage…" he faltered and chose more diplomatic words, "the differences between you and Julie."

"That's bad enough. They don't realise."

"Don't realise what?"

"What the ice melt could mean."

"Well, what could it mean?"

"Ultimately death, destruction chaos."

"Ice melt?"

"Yeah, in the Arctic and elsewhere. Greenland. I've been there and seen for myself and had the science explain all that water from the ice melt. You know what it means?"

"I think I have some idea…I read the *Guardian* as well…"

He is interrupted by Mark, "But do you know what it really means?"

"I suppose like you said but I don't follow…"

Again Mark interrupted, "Flooding, torrents of water coming down the North Sea down every river mouth on the eastern coast of the UK. To the Thames and if the storm's big enough over the Thames Barrier. And…" He falters.

"Phew, that's something else but haven't they got provision for such an event?"

"That's just it. If they don't fully acknowledge the situation, then there's no need to provide what's required."

"I'm sure they're not that naive. There must be some arrangements. It's happened before surely."

"Yeah, it has. My own grandfather was involved in the Canvey Island floods in 1953. He got away with his life—a lot didn't. The next one is going to make that look like a picnic." He paused.

"Bloody hell, that sounds bad."

"Yeah, I'm trying to explain to Julie that if it happens. If water surges down the Thames, all our lives will be fucked. So far, I haven't got this over to her. You know how it is—you articulate these reasons after you've left the house."

"Do you think she will understand even if you put it like that?"

"I don't know—maybe."

Jake picked up his pint, took a drink and looked around the pub not really seeing the scene but engrossed in thoughts of how to help his friend.

"You see, Jake if you get a surge…" he faltered. "You don't want to hear all that stuff."

"No, go on. Tell me." The pub was beginning to fill up with people and noise was increasing with an air of bonhomie as people ordered their drinks and found places to sit or stand to talk. Mark leaned closer to Jake so that he could be heard more clearly.

"Well, having gone to the Metrological Centre and The Environmental Agency and various university research departments which specialise in climate change and climatology, the conclusions are that many cities around the world are under threat of flooding including London."

"I could imagine it will be pretty bad," said Jake with understatement.

"Pretty bad? It'll be disastrous! If a tidal wave comes down the Thames, it will sweep everything before it. It'll hit the docklands, City of London, Central London, even the Houses of Parliament and it won't stop until its energy is dissipated. Just think, Jake, 52 underground stations will be potentially under threat from flooding and those nearest the Thames to flooding of catastrophic levels."

"Surely the authorities have made provision for this kind of thing?" Jake said incredulously.

"Well, yeah. Kind of. I talked to the Environmental Agency, The River Authority and London Transport the lot. Yeah, they have some arrangements but I'm afraid, my friend, they will be pitifully inadequate. Even they admit it."

"They are aware?"

"Oh, yeah. Painfully aware."

"Well, why don't they do more?"

"Money. Resources. Since the crash of 2007–8, austerity has been the name of the game and there's just not the cash to make appropriate provision."

"But they know how bad it could be and still do nothing?"

"Well, the experts know there is a problem but there's no political will. You have to convince the politicians. And with this lot in power well…quite a few deny climate change and the rest rarely think about it as an issue."

"Until that is it hits them in the face," Jake interjected.

"Yeah, exactly! But to give them their due, nobody knows when this might happen. Next week, next year, ten, twenty, thirty years' time. All we know is that as each day passes and the ice melts and the climate becomes more unpredictable, the chances of it happening increase every day."

"And you think your articles can help spread the bad news?"

"Yeah, it is bad news," said Mark, "but I've got to get the message to as wide an audience as possible. I have had articles in specialist journals and news sheets of Green Peace and other eco organisations but we have to get it to those that read mainstream stuff."

"And get it on social media," interjected Jake.

"Yeah, that's increasingly important. That gets it to the younger folk but the oldies don't really believe in the potential danger and some don't even care, and they are the people holding the reins of power. Most may well be dead before anything happens."

"Surely, that's a bit cynical 'oldies don't care'," said Jake.

"Well, some do care as there are some youngsters not interested in the issue. But they are all affected."

"What about these hurricanes in the Caribbean and the USA? Even the BBC are asking experts whether they are connected to climate change."

"Yeah, it's got to be connected. The strength and close repetition of the hurricanes are something new. I and many others think these are symptoms of fast-changing weather patterns brought on by industrial pollution and other factors caused by humans. Take temperature change—the Earth has heated up more rapidly in the past 100 years than the last 3,000 years. Even in geological time terms, that's unusual."

Chapter 8
The Environment Agency

Mark approached the Department of Environment Food and Rural Affairs building. Its stone-clad entrance hinted at modest pretensions to classical architecture. It was not in the same league in terms of grandiosity as ministry buildings in Parliament Street, but it was impressive enough and caused him some trepidation as he pushed through the doors of Ergon House. He had managed to get an interview with a senior official of the Environment Agency who had phoned him yesterday to say that the arranged interview was not going to be with him but with a junior member of the department who specialised in flood control matters. His name apparently was Dominic Harris.

He approached the desk and was made to wait a minute or so while the receptionist finished looking through a file. He finally lifted his head. "How can I help you?" He said without a hint of facial expression.

"I have an appointment to see Dominic Harris."

"If you take a seat, I will call his office," the receptionist said while lifting the phone to his ear. "A gentleman to see Dominic Harris. Right." He replaced the phone on its cradle. "He will be down to meet you shortly."

Mark looked around the vestibule area and thought that this bureaucracy was trying vainly to become part of the twenty-first century. Competing with and attempting to emulate the large global corporations whose budgets dwarfed the ministry. The endeavours had failed as the modernisation programmes were severely affected by austerity cuts which had swept through Westminster.

He took out a folder from his bag and began to pass the time by boning up on some of the questions he had prepared. After a couple of minutes, a man emerged from a lift and strode purposely toward him. "Dominic Harris," he said holding out his hand. Mark stood and shook his hand.

"We'll go to a break-out room on the second floor if you follow me." Mark followed him into the lift to the second floor where they emerged into a corridor. Mark followed him past several doors until Dominic Harris stopped, took out a key and ushered Mark ahead of him into a sparsely furnished room containing only a couple of chairs and a table.

"Please, take a seat and call me Dominic. We are trying to reduce the formalities."

"No problem. I'm Mark." Dominic held out his hand for Mark to take a chair and instead of sitting opposite the table as if in an interview situation, he pulled a chair round to sit beside Mark. "Hopefully, we can lessen the air of officialdom."

"How can I help you? I believe you are interested in matters relating to climate change."

"Yes, I'm a freelance journalist specialising in environmental issues. As I understand it, Dominic, you are quite an expert on flood control. I'm interested to know how vulnerable London is to such an event."

"I assume you mean flooding?"

"Precisely."

"What exactly do you know about the subject?" Dominic said.

"Well, my father and grandfather were involved in the Canvey Island floods of 1953 and they were forced out of their homes and I know that with rising sea levels, a lot of cities are under threat from flooding, including London. Could another Canvey be avoided?"

"That depends on many factors. The strength of a sea surge, whether this is accompanied by tidal swelling due to rainfall, the time over which such incidents take place."

"Let's take one incident at a time," suggested Mark. "What impact would a sea surge have on the Thames, for example?"

"I am sure you are aware that with ice melt in the Northern Hemisphere, seas are bound to rise. Reports from the Meteorological Office and environmental science research groups are uncertain as to the precise speed of the ice melt but we do know that it's happening faster than we had previously thought."

Mark nodded. "Yes, I have visited many ice research posts based in Greenland and elsewhere. The increased pace of ice and glacier melt is alarming many in the climate research community. I also know that this could enhance any storm surge in the North Sea. What I want to know is what impact that will have on London if, for example, the Thames Barrier is breached?"

"A number of reports were produced by The Environment Agency and Transport for London…"

"Yes, but I have read the most recent one by London Underground," said Mark before Dominic could finish. He didn't want to be brushed off by a smooth-talking official. He wanted the bald and perhaps unedifying truth.

Dominic looked closely at Mark and said, "The fact is LU's report can only be described as alarming. It states, and the EA agrees, that as many as 57 London Underground stations are at high risk of flooding. Most threatened are the capital's busiest stations, including Waterloo, Kings Cross and London Bridge. This will be of considerable danger to members of the travelling public."

Mark knew most of this but it came as a shock when said out loud by a government official.

"The Report was commissioned by LU after the flooding of the New York metro system caused by Hurricane Sandy in 2012. Three and half million people use the London Underground system daily."

"This could be potentially disastrous," Mark interjected.

"I would suggest the word catastrophic," Dominic said rather too soberly for Mark.

"Typical British understatement," thought Mark, but to his surprise, Dominic leaned forward and almost in a conspiratorial voice and said, "Little has been done. The London Mayor's Office published a report on this subject in October 2011."

"When Boris Johnson was in office?"

"Exactly. The report was noted but not acted on. In fact, the situation has got even worse with the cuts in budgets of LU, the EA and other bodies. The austerity measures introduced since 2010 have witnessed cuts, sometimes savage cuts in the operating personnel of the emergency services and that includes police, health service, fire service, air-sea rescue and so on."

"So things could be even worse than the LU report suggests?" Mark said incredulously.

"Oh, yes. We thought the government had a wake-up call when there were extensive floods in the West Country and Cumbria. In 2013, when the Somerset Levels flooded badly, it was revealed that the cutbacks in the EA funding meant that even less could be done to help the waterlogged residents. A long-term solution is needed and that means planning and investment, but of course, planning had never been popular with Tory governments since Thatcher and public spending was always to be resisted. It was only because it was the heartland of a Tory voting area that Cameron panicked and began to suggest schemes."

"Such as dredging the rivers flowing from the region to the Bristol Channel," Mark interjected.

"Yes, and the government had to spend an extra £30 million in repairs. All very short-termist and locking the stable door after the horse has bolted."

"And dredging rivers may not be an answer?"

"All too true. Like most things in this area of science, there is still a lot of speculation. But one thing we know for sure is that there is going to be more flooding. Take the Thames, for example. It's not only prone to sea surges at the estuary but also prolonged heavy rainfall inland. If it rains heavily in Oxfordshire and the home counties, it will ultimately make its way to the Thames and create flooding. In prolonged heavy rain scenarios, a rise of several metres may cause a tidal surge."

"So what if a sea surge and a tidal surge happen at the same time?" Mark asked.

"Well, a disaster of colossal proportions," Dominic said almost blandly.

"It doesn't bear thinking about. But what measures are in place in the case of such an event?"

Chapter 9
The Storm Cometh

On the far side of the Atlantic Ocean in the Caribbean, a hurricane of gigantic proportions was moving its way slowly towards the North American mainland. It was not the first to hit the already devastated islands in this season of storms. But Hurricane Betsy was set to dwarf all previous tempests as its funnelling winds swept through the defenceless Caribbean Islands wreaking devastation to all things in its path. Flimsy buildings made of timber and plasterboard were swept aside like matchwood. Even the more substantial buildings began to sway in thrall to its power. 12 September 2026 was going to be a memorable date and not in a good way.

Mike Pennington, head of the US National Hurricane Centre in Florida turned to his colleague Simon Schwartz.

"This looks like a biggie, we need to alert all agencies including the President."

"I'll get on to the medical crews, police and…"

"You'd better get in contact with the armed forces as well."

"You think it'll be that bad?" Simon asked incredulously.

"Yeah, think disaster on a big scale. This is gonna be a potential catastrophe!"

"Hey, look over here," Jane Collier yelled. Her job was to track the hurricane's path. They rushed over to the large computer screen on the wall in front of her desk. "Wow," both said in unison. A massive swirling image was moving slowly along a map of the east coast of the USA and heading straight for Florida.

"When do you think it'll make the US mainland?" Simon asked.

"It's hard to tell. They often move at varying speeds depending on weather conditions but I should say between 12 and 24 hours," Jane said concentrating hard on the satellite image on the screen.

"We knew it was going to be a big storm over a week ago, but nothing like this. It could be devastating."

"Yeah, it could and it probably will be. Did you contact the armed forces, Simon?"

"I'm on it."

"Torrential rain has already hit the Keys and is moving rapidly north," Jane pointed to the screen. "If that continues and gets above 30 inches, we're in for flash flooding or worse."

"We need to contact all emergency managers and security agents in adjacent states. Louisiana, Georgia and South Carolina," Mike said looking in grim concentration at the satellite image on the screen which showed a white pulsating swirling mass moving slowly towards the coast of South Florida.

"It's moving faster than we thought," Jane said.

"We need to ensure the emergency services have evacuation procedures ready to roll."

"They'll have a hard time, no matter how well prepared they are."

"This is Mika Brzezinski with NBC breaking news at 5:30 p.m. on 12 September:

"Reports are coming in from the National Weather Service and other coastal agencies. Hurricane Betsy is heading rapidly towards the eastern seaboard with the first landfall being the South Florida mainland. The storm already being hailed by experts as the largest they have experienced has wreaked havoc in the Caribbean. With an estimated thousand people killed and thousands more homeless and missing as winds of up to 200 mph have smashed homes and public utilities. A national emergency has been announced. Leaders in Caribbean states are declaring disaster zones and calling on the international community for help.

Residents in Miami and other cities and towns in the southeast coastal seaboard are advised to evacuate their homes or ensure their safety in protected places. All emergency services are on the alert and a state of emergency has been declared by the President.

"The Governor of Florida Bill Harvey has urged immediate evacuation of communities on the coast. He also stated that it was not voluntary but mandatory, and those who did not comply would put themselves in great danger. All government buildings will be closed including schools and colleges in coastal counties."

Similar messages are coming from state governors and senators in Georgia and the Carolinas.

For some background to these increasing extreme weather conditions, we have been talking to Dr Richard Burkhardt from the National Oceanic and Atmospheric Administration.

"Dr Burkhardt, what do you think are the principal causes of these recent extreme weather events?"

"An extreme weather event such as Betsy has been on the cards for some years. Meteorologists have been monitoring increasingly severe storm systems. The first signs came with Hurricane Katrina in 2005 and there has been increasing frequency and intensity of hurricane events since then."

"Yes, but what are the causes?"

"In a nutshell, global warming, or as we scientists prefer to call it climate change. The greenhouse gases we have pumped into the atmosphere over the last two centuries have caused the earth to heat up. In turn, the seas have been warming with huge ice melts in Greenland. Also discovered in 2019 was the massive melt of Thwaites Glacier in Antarctica. These are causing the seas to rise…"

"But how does that lead to massive hurricanes?"

"Well, as white ice and snow turn to dark sea water, the heating effect increases as darker surfaces don't reflect the heat, they absorb it. Warmer seas intensify weather changes and create a higher likelihood of severe cyclonic events and storm surges."

"So the hotter the planet gets the more likely we have the possibility of extreme weather events like Betsy."

"Yeah, and I am pretty certain there will be another one close after."

"Another one?"

"It's highly possible."

"On that worrying note, thank you, Dr Burkhardt."

Mika turns to camera 2.

"We have with us in the studio Reverend William Jones who like many Republicans holds contrary views to Dr Burkhardt on climate change. Reverend Jones, why do you think climate change is a fantasy and what do you think caused these extreme weather events?"

"Firstly, the climate change advocates are highly political and are just jumping on the bandwagon to keep Republicans out of the Senate in the coming elections."

"But what do you think caused this rush of hurricanes over the past years?"

"I admit that things are seemingly getting extreme at times, but these events are cyclical. The good Lord in his wisdom has made these changes from time to time. I believe they are sent to punish us for our wickedness."

"So you have no truck with the idea that these events are a result of increased greenhouse gases released into the atmosphere?"

"The weather is something only God can influence. It is something beyond our control. We are in the hands of God."

"But what about the scientific evidence? It seems to overwhelmingly back the view that climate change is coming and it's manmade!"

"These so-called scientists are in the pay of the Democrats, liberals and communists. There is no truth in these so-called facts."

"Fake news?"

"Fake news it definitely is."

"Thanks, Reverend. Well, one thing's for sure, the storm is heading our way. Let's hope it blows itself out before then."

At the US Hurricane Centre, Jane Collier switched off the office TV in disgust.

"Did you hear that arsehole? It's God's punishment. It makes you wonder what we're doing here."

"You don't have to be an agnostic or atheist to believe that climate change is manmade. I regularly attend our local church and many folks who worship there are on our side. These evangelists are extremists full of ego and self-promotion," said Mike Pennington.

"Why the hell do they have these nutty guys on a big channel like NBC?"

"They want controversy and what they call 'lively debate'," said Mike.

"Fuck 'em! Let's see what Betsy's been doing," Simon said emphatically turning to his data screen.

The South Coast Trailer Park is nestled inland from the Florida coast 20 miles south of Miami. It was made up of holiday homes and some permanent residents who could not afford a more substantial dwelling. Some called them 'trailer trash' but for anyone who visited these parks, they were made up of regular decent folk making a go of things and trying to get along although not always succeeding. Jesse and Tracy Jackson had moved down to the park 10 years earlier upping sticks from Flint Michigan, looking for sun, sand, sea and a better life. It wasn't exactly the 'promised land' they'd hoped for. Trailer park life could be tough when income was low and reliance on welfare and a small pension was their only hope. But they made the best of it and even tried to help the less fortunate who inhabited some of the more run-down parts of the site which the owners had failed to maintain. They wanted your rent pronto but the repairs were very slow in coming.

Their trailer was comfortable enough with a long lounge, shower and bathroom, a large and small bedroom and a medium-sized living room lavishly furnished with a thick carpet with a bright red tiger imprinted on it. Colour pictures of Jesus and small statuettes and other nick-knacks collected over the years peppered the room. Photographs of their son, daughter and grandchildren stood on a side cupboard. They didn't often see them these days as Gary lived in California and Jackie in Chicago. They saw their two grandchildren once a year when Jackie brought them down to stay. The kids loved the beaches and the sun. Quite a contrast to their city life. Gary phoned occasionally and kept in touch by Facebook but he had been in and out of a number of relationships and seemed unable to stay for long with one partner.

"I'm gonna get down there one day," Gary often told his parents.

"Yeah, that'll be the day," Jesse commented dryly after Tracy signed off from Facebook. Jesse sighed, picked up the remote of their large TV and clicked it on.

"Let's see what the weather's been doing."

"It's getting mighty windy outside. That storm seems to be blowing up our way pretty quickly."

"Quicker than they thought," said Jesse staring at the large screen showing a weather map with symbols of swirling winds eddying their way up the Florida coast.

He turned the volume up and the presenter's voice filled the room.

"Hurricane Betsy is now heading towards the United States and will hit the Florida coast in four hours. Experts at meteorological stations are predicting winds as high as 120 mph or more and very high seas. The state authorities are requesting that people in homes especially near the coast should leave and seek refuge in community centres such as schools, churches and public halls. There will be beds and food available until the storm passes over."

"Do you think we ought to do as they say?" Tracy said in a concerned voice.

"Well, we lasted out all the storms over the past ten years so I reckon we could with this Betsy. OK, we had to do some repairs but our little old trailer took the strain."

"Yeah, but they are saying this one's going to be really big." As if to emphasise Tracy's words, a large gust of wind shook the trailer.

"We'll just hunker down and see this thing out. We've enough food and drink and I certainly don't want to sleep on a high school gym floor for God knows how many nights."

"I suppose you're right, Jesse, but I'm scared."

Mike Schwartz and Jane Collier turned to the office TV to catch the latest news items to which they themselves, as part of the National Hurricane Centre, had been contributors.

"Ex-President Trump on one of his many visits to his Miami luxury home at Mar-a-Lago in Palm Beach has been grounded. He had hoped to return to New York and leave the storm behind but all aircraft are forbidden to fly as the storm begins to reach its peak and will make landfall very soon. The ex-President says he is not worried as his Mar-a-Lago home is pretty solid. They'll wait out the storm like all the other Florida folk. In 2005, the 126-room building was damaged by storms and an insurance claim of $17 million was filed by the Trump estate. At that time, the sea had flooded the estate leaving a number of buildings partially under water. High winds had blown parts of the roofing off and had to be repaired."

"Well, that's ironic! The arch climate change denier caught by a storm caused by climate change."

"Well, Jane, he can't do any harm now that he's out of office," Mike said.

"I do hope he doesn't drown," Simon said with an enormous grin.

"Now, now, folks, we're supposed to be neutral in the political area."

"Just a few private thoughts, Mike."

They returned to their workstations happy that they had discovered some humour in this potential disaster.

Tracy watched out of the window as their neighbours filed out of the trailer park in their cars and trucks, stuffed with clothing, bedding, pets, food and drink and anything they considered important. Jesse stood on his trailer porch buffeted by the rising winds but standing stalwart and defiant.

One of the trucks stopped and a man in a Stetson hat and a long droopy moustache called out in the wind. "Ain't you coming, Jesse?"

"Naw, we'll be fine. We've stuck it out for the last ten years and we'll stick this one out as well."

"Well, good luck, my friend, and hope to see you when this blows over."

"Yeah," said Jesse waving his hand.

The wind began to blow harder and Jesse watched as the last truck left the trailer park. He felt somewhat dejected knowing that he and Tracy were the only ones left. He hurried inside as the winds increased, and had a hard time closing the trailer door, as the wind whipped across the park. He locked and bolted the door. Tracy came and stood beside him and held his arm.

"I hope you're right about this, hon."

"We're OK. Put some coffee on."

Jesse slumped into an armchair and adjusted his large T-shirt which just about covered his belly. He too had some misgivings now he had time to contemplate. He brushed his hand over his thinning hair and wiped away some beads of sweat.

"Here you are, hun," Tracy said handing him a mug of coffee.

Just then the gloomy sky began to darken and they heard the first drops of rain hit the roof of the trailer. Soon the intensity of the rain and wind increased.

They heard the clattering of loose objects outside being buffeted by the wind. A large plastic bin whirled passed their door and smashed against the trailer next door.

Trying to reassure the obvious disquiet he could see on Tracy's face, he said, "Let's put the TV on and watch a show, and try to forget about it."

When he pressed the remote, a fizzing screen greeted him. He played around with the buttons for a while but with little result. *Must be the satellite dish*, he thought. He looked out of the window. Hanging from the roof was a long cable on the end of which was a bent satellite dish.

"Sweet Jesus. No TV. What will we do now?" He tried the radio and heard a crackling voice.

"At least, that's working, Tracy. We can keep up with what's happening."

"I can see what's happening by looking out of the window," Tracy said in a voice verging on the shrill. As if to emphasise her words, hard rain hit the roof and sides of their trailer buffeting it to the point where they felt it had moved.

Jesse adjusted the radio reception and a clearer voice emerged. "Hurricane Betsy is now very close to the Florida mainland and people will be experiencing its full force very soon. All government agencies have warned all residents to evacuate their homes and move as far from the coast as possible. It's predicted that flash flooding and water rises of considerable size are inevitable."

"That doesn't sound too good but we'll be fine," Jesse said with a little quaver in his voice. He adjusted the radio to find some music and the reassuring sounds of a country band filled the room.

In the next half hour, winds pounded and pummelled the trailer park. Objects flew past their window and the rain almost horizontal from the high wind, struck their home forcefully. The sound was quite deafening as if a million ants in heavy boots were marching up and down the roof and sides at great speed. Doors and windows rattled, and the porch roof shook so much it seemed it might fly off at any moment.

Then there was a slowing down of the wind and the rain and after ten minutes there was comparative silence and the sky cleared.

"Looks like it's blown over," Jesse said reassuringly.

"Mmmm," Tracy didn't sound convinced. "It could be the eye of the storm."

Jesse got up. "I'm gonna take a look." He unlocked the door and went outside on the porch. There was debris everywhere and one of the more flimsy trailers had blown apart and another was keeled over on its side. Tracy had gingerly slipped out to join him.

"I don't believe it," Jesse said. "Looks like Emmy Lou's home has been wrecked good and proper."

"What will she do, Jesse, now she ain't got a home?"

"Only the good Lord knows."

Suddenly the wind began to blow stronger and the rain began again. They hurried inside and quickly secured the door.

The wind increased in speed and howled through the telephone wires. The poles began to shake. Large debris hit the wires which caused them to come crashing down onto their trailer roof.

"Oh my God, Jesse, what was that?" Tracy yelled in alarm. They both looked up at a telephone pole which had made a hole in their roof. Rain began to splash down on their tiger carpet and within five minutes, it was sodden.

Chapter 10
Hell Hath No Fury

At the Hurricane Centre in Miami, Jane put down the phone. "Mike, there's a reporter who wants an interview about the storm."

"We're pretty busy but I suppose I can spare a moment," Mike replied. "I'll phone back."

"No need, she's at reception," Jane looked amusingly resigned.

"OK, send her up."

Five minutes later, Deborah Steinberger appeared at their control room door already wearing a security tag.

"Hi. Mike Pennington, Director for The National Hurricane Centre."

"Deborah Steinberger, *Miami Herald*. Thanks for taking the time out to see me."

"Take a seat. Coffee?"

"No thanks." Deborah sat down on a padded chair flicked back her long blonde hair and put her laptop on the table in front of her. Then she rifled in her bag for her phone. Accessed the recorder and was just about to press the red button when she said, "I hope it's OK?" Her vivid blue eyes stared into Mike's face.

Mike taken aback a little, blurted, "Sure. Go ahead?"

Deborah didn't waste time and launched straight in. "It seems these storms are getting more frequent and stronger and more dangerous. Would you say that was true?"

"It's undoubtedly the case. Storms have been increasing in number and frequency over the last 10 years as you must know. There were 31 named storms across the United States last year and eight were considered major and categorised as four or five."

"Is five the highest category?"

"It sure is and if things get any worse we may have to extend that category to six." He laughed at his own attempt at humour. Deborah stayed straight-faced and looked at him with her piercing eyes as if to say this is no time for jokes. A little uncomfortable, Mike ploughed on. "Hurricanes and storms in the past produced high winds of 120 mph and often more but in 2019 the first 200 mph winds were repeatedly recorded."

"What does this mean for the USA and more particularly Florida and the eastern seaboard?" She pushed her phone towards Mike as if this was the main answer she had been searching for.

"This is strongly related to the recording of the hottest and wettest years on records in the past decade, in fact since records were accurately kept in the mid-nineteenth century."

"But that storm's going crazy out there. Homes are being washed away and huge waves are pounding the shoreline and flooding inland. Rivers are swollen and swamping towns and cities."

"I am afraid all this was predictable and climate scientists have been warning politicians and the general public for years but relatively little has been done. This storm for instance was predicted and monitored and now it's getting bigger as it makes landfall."

"Can anything be done now?"

"Yes and no!"

"What do you mean?"

"It's too late to reverse global warming to any extent and we will just have to cope with the storm with the resources we have, but we could take stronger measures for the long term. Stop burning fossil fuels entirely, for example."

"But people are suffering now."

"The emergency services just aren't given enough money and resources to cope with these kind of situations. Money should have poured in long ago and tighter arrangements and planning made. But we have to live with what we've got and to be honest, it will be about trying to save lives. Properties will have to wait until it's all over. This means adapting to changing conditions."

"Such as?"

"In the long term, moving people away from flood plains, having more eco-friendly transport that doesn't burn fossil fuels, preserving the planet's natural environment. I could go on all day."

"But for now?"

"We do the best we can."

A mobile began to ring. It was ringing inside her bag. "Excuse me," she said taking it out and pressing the answer button. Mike turned to look at the data screens as if not to overhear the phone conversation.

After a few nods of the head, Deborah ended the call. "Thanks for your information, Mike, but I'll have to go. They want me to cover the story at ground level. You know get down and dirty. Meet the flood victims and all that."

"Well, good luck with that," Mike said to Deborah's back as she rushed out of the Hurricane Centre control room.

Deborah drove with her cameraman to the Miami coast where the storm was fiercest. The wind was now blowing frantically. Cars and trucks lay abandoned along the highway. They parked on the edge of the city and entered an apartment block which seemed to sway in the wind. "Let's get some shelter from the storm here. Get up high so we can get a much better view of the situation."

They rode the elevator to the tenth floor of the building and emerged onto a corridor with apartment entrances on one side and large picture windows on the other. They walked to the end of the corridor until they had a view of the coast and the city. There was no sign of any residents.

The scene below looked like a battlefield. The wind was racing so fast they could feel the tower block shudder. The sea was very high and appeared to be moving inland fast.

Looking down, they saw two cars keel over in the wind as a desperate driver tried to drive out of the area. The wind blew it into another car and they both rolled over and down onto the beach where they were quickly covered by a large wave. The drivers didn't stand a chance. Lance, her cameraman, was clicking away.

"Did you see that?" Deborah said visibly shaken. She got out her cell phone. "We ought to call the emergency services." Almost immediately, the call was answered. Deborah explained what she had seen. Then listened intently for a while and said, "So you can't do anything for that guy?" She switched off the call in disgust.

"What'd he say?" Lance said.

"Their emergency services are all tied up and can do little at the height of the storm. He said everyone had been advised not to go out but there's always someone who'll ignore the warnings."

After ten minutes of observation and taking notes and pictures, Lance let the camera drop to his chest and ran his fingers through his sleek black hair. "We got some great shots but we can't stay here. It's too dangerous."

"We should be OK. This building is pretty solid and anyway, I need some interviews. Some quotes," said Deborah.

Deborah walked down the corridor and pounded on a few doors but there was no response. The building seemed deserted. Finally one of the doors opened and a thin man in his seventies said, "Yeah? What do you want?"

"Hi, I'm from the *Miami Herald* and was wondering if you could tell us why you're still here and how you are coping with the storm?"

"I seem to be the only one left in the block. Do you want to come in for some coffee?" The man seemed grateful for the company. They entered the apartment which was clean and tidy but rather sparse in terms of furniture and adornments.

"Thanks," said Deborah, "do you have a table I can use to send a report back to my paper?" He showed her and Lance into a living room where a table and two upright chairs were placed by a small table. "Take a seat. I'll go make the coffee." The man had a New York accent. Deborah opened her laptop and began to file the report and then she downloaded some of Lance's pictures and sent them off.

The man returned with two coffee cups. "Black, OK? I don't have any milk or cream. I went out to get some but had to go a long way as all the local stores were boarded up. I found nothing and decided to come back. Oh boy, that was an experience. By the time I got back, people had left or were leaving the building."

"So why didn't you join them?" Deborah asked.

"Well, I'm on my own now. I got enough food and stuff and I prefer my own company. But I'm glad to see you guys. Experiencing this storm on your own ain't no fun. I'm beginning to think I should have joined the neighbours."

As they drank, they could feel the wind getting stronger. It was pushing against the window as if at any moment they might cave in. They got up and looked out of the window. Debris was flying everywhere and the coast road adjacent to the beach was now underwater.

"You don't want to be out in that. You could get killed," the man said laconically.

"Well, we've got to try to get back somehow," Deborah said.

Just then the electric lights went off. Lance went outside the apartment and rushed to the elevator. He pressed the button frantically, but it was no longer working.

"We'll have to leg it down the stairs I'm afraid," Lance said.

They heard the sound of a huge wave crashing into the building. They rushed to one of the windows overlooking the coast and looked down. "God, we'll never get out of here," Deborah said in alarm, more concerned about not getting her stories for the next edition filed.

"It doesn't look like you'll be going nowhere for a while," said the old man leaning against his front door.

In Miami, there was chaos in the streets with overturned cars, trucks and garbage cans being lifted into the air crashing down bending panels and crushing bonnets. Water quickly rushed over the vehicles taking them off in the tide as if a new fast-flowing river had been born. Drains and sewers unable to cope with the huge amounts of water were deluged and finally hidden in the flood. The water developed fast currents with the heavy wind and animals and people could be seen struggling to save themselves but to no avail. Their wails and cries were lost in the wind and with arms flailing were swept away.

Shops, restaurants and main street businesses were flooded. The muddy water swirled around their floors and people watched horrified and traumatised. Water levels were now over three feet and rising. People were hanging out of windows above ground floor level.

The winds were so strong that all aircraft were grounded and there was no way the emergency services could reach these victims. Police and firefighters themselves were washed away. It was often a case of saving themselves let alone others.

At the Federal Emergency Management Agency (FEMA), local headquarters Lieutenant Colonel James 'Chuck' Aldred was attempting to make meaning of the situation and direct what forces were available to areas of the greatest need.

The local office situated in Miami was as much affected as any other buildings in the city.

Chuck was on the phone to the FEMA's national HQ in Washington, DC. He emphasised to his chief General Barker, "We'll do what we can, Sir. That's all we can do in the situation. We've not seen anything on this scale before and that has been confirmed by Mike Pennington over in the Hurricane Centre. He also thinks things could get worse."

"What do you mean worse, Chuck?" General Barker replied rather sharply.

"Well, in all my military experience…" He stalled unable to evoke the right words, "Sir, I think this is a whole new ball game. Things seem to be falling apart. Emergency services can't get through. To be frank, Sir, it's chaos out there."

"I'll have to contact the President there is nothing for it. We must declare a national emergency and use all means at our disposal."

"Information from Mike Pennington sees the storm increasing in ferocity but it will blow out and move out into the Atlantic, but that won't be for at least 24 hours, Sir."

"Do the best you can, Chuck."

"I will, Sir," and with that, the phone went dead.

Over the next 24 hours, the storm raged. Miami was flooded. There was wreckage everywhere. Hundreds of people sought refuge and hundreds died. It was the worst storm experienced by Florida in its recorded history.

At Mar-a-Lago, ex-President Trump was marooned in his massive country retreat. The gardens were completely inundated and the ground floors were underwater. Thousands of tiles had been ripped from the roof and rainwater had penetrated into the upper exposed floors. Trees in the surrounding parklands had been uprooted and the swimming pools were awash with seawater and sewage. The golf course was completely deluged.

When it was all over and the emergency services could finally get through, Trump was cold, wet, shaken and physically ill. He was flown to New York and treated in a private hospital special unit where he died three days later.

They found Jesse and Tracy four days later lying dead in the wreckage of their trailer. It seemed not one piece of their home lay intact. The storm had devastated the whole of The South Coast Trailer Park and many other such parks dotted along the Florida coast.

Deborah and Lance after 24 hours were able to leave the apartment block. They had more than enough comment from the elderly man who seemed to enjoy their company enormously although the two reporters could not reciprocate the feeling. They were glad to get away and were alive and able to file several stories before they gingerly let themselves out into what looked like a war zone.

The President declared South Florida a disaster area, and the emergency services began the long and painful task of finding dead bodies and burying them, as well as rescuing anyone left alive. Much of Miami lay underwater. Recovery was going to be a long haul. Any doubts about climate change died with the storm.

Chapter 11
West Coast

Dingle being one of the most westerly towns on the West Coast of the Republic of Ireland was usually the first to be hit by storms from the Atlantic, depending on the winds and position of incoming depressions. The small fishing port with a population of just above 2,000 people lay on the northern head of Dingle Bay. It had become a notable fishing port from the nineteenth century when mackerel and herring were fished from there.

The O'Connor and Cavanagh families had long relied on the fishing trade to earn a living in Dingle and they shared a trawler and scraped a living from fishing the Atlantic waters. John O'Connor normally skippered the boat and Liam Cavanagh acted as his second-in-command, although they often reversed roles. It seemed to work for them although there were the occasional disagreements.

Their boat was a wet fish trawler which had no freezing equipment to preserve the caught fish. This meant they could not venture far out to sea and the duration of their expeditions would usually last from 36 to 48 hours, maybe longer, depending on weather conditions and market requirements. Regular trips were a feature of their business when conditions allowed but the need for rapid turnover of fish and cash in exchange was imperative as they had numerous expenses, the main one being the loan payments on their £250,000 trawler *Lucy Ann*.

They were proud of their boat and generally, they liked the fishing life although at times, it could be boring, and by contrast, dangerous. John O'Connor was a large, self-confident man with a thick wave of blond hair and broad shoulders. He liked to be in control but would concede to his friend and partner Liam Cavanagh when Liam insisted he needed rest, and on long fishing trips, rest was not always easy to get. Liam, a shorter man going bald with greying hair on his temples and a lined face, was much quieter and more cautious. The two men sometimes had disagreements when John wanted to do something which Liam thought was risky and or unnecessary. Generally, John got his way.

Their other two crew members were John's son Patrick and Billy Maguire who had only been a crew member for six months but had soon learned the way of things not only as a trawlerman but as a member of the crew.

It was 20 September 2026; the weather had been fair and John and Liam agreed they could take out 'Lucy Ann' before Storm Betsy crossed the Atlantic. Although they usually got the tail end of the hurricanes which came from the Caribbean and the Eastern Seaboard of the United States, the winds usually blew themselves out by mid-Atlantic. Nevertheless, the winds could be quite fresh when they finally hit the Irish coast creating some pretty nasty storms. This has increasingly been the case in the last few years. The storms had been stronger and had caused quite heavy rain coming from the deep Atlantic depressions as they travelled eastwards to the British Isles. But the communities had borne them with fortitude and a sense of the inevitable. There was nothing for it but to stay at home and shelter until the storms had passed.

Fishing was the good life on a fine day but there was very little shelter on board the deck of a trawler and when the weather turned round, things could easily roll from heaven to hell, sometimes in the wink of an eye.

The 'Lucy Ann' chugged steadily through the rising and falling waves. The green ocean turned white as it spumed and frothed in the wake of the boat. They hauled up one of the nets and examined the contents. "It's a little short of what we need. Let's put it over again," said John shaking his head in disappointment.

"It'll do. Why risk our necks with this storm coming?" Liam said.

"Aw, that'll blow itself out long before we finish here. They always do."

"I'm not a gambling man, John, and I don't like the thought of taking a risk unnecessarily." Liam puffed on a cigarette and looked at the catch. "It's not great but it's enough."

"One more catch and we'll get a good return. I need the money."

Liam looked at John with a smile of bitter resignation. "We all need it, John."

They'd been fishing off the Skelligs and the Blasket Islands and one more catch would mean a trawl of several hours maybe longer. Patrick remained quiet and Billy gazed down at his rubber boots and assumed a face of resignation. It seemed neither was easy with this extra duty. They had heard the news of Storm Betsy and they didn't like it one little bit. Patrick finally decided to raise the unspoken question, "Da don't you think it's too risky? These storms are getting worse year by year."

"I've been on the boats for the past 30 years and I'm telling you, son, we'll be fine."

"I just hope you're right, da." Patrick strode back to the fish holds. Billy went to the prow and began disentangling some ropes which had been twisted. All distractions while John got his way.

"Why don't you go the galley and make yourself a coffee? You could get me one too."

Liam walked unenthusiastically inside and put the kettle on to boil. While it boiled, he turned on the radio and got a local station. Some music drifted through the boat although most was drowned out by the noise of the increasingly turbulent sea. He made a coffee and called Patrick and Billy. The radio DJ said, "And now here is the latest track from our very own Pauline Scanlon singing 'The Old Churchyard' from her bestselling album 'Gossamer'." The beautiful voice filled the galley and Liam sat down to listen intently.

When the music finished, the DJ said, "And now a weather report." Liam sat upright and turned up the volume. "Hurricane Betsy has travelled up the east coast of USA and is now set to cross the Atlantic. Generally, these hurricanes blow themselves out by mid-Atlantic although expect quite heavy winds and rain. Temperatures are average for this time of the year."

Liam picked up his coffee, took a sip and began to contemplate what he had just heard. Maybe John was right after all. Maybe it will blow itself out. Liam took coffees out to John, Patrick and Billy and repeated the forecast news. They all grinned their approval. They were on for another trawl.

They chugged along for another couple of hours moving further out to sea. The boat began to rock more decisively as it pushed its way through the increasingly choppy waters. The larger swells of the sea began to make the crew members a little uneasy. Even John began to look with concern at the far western horizon puffing on yet another cigarette.

Liam approached him on the bridge and John turned to face him holding the ship as steady as he could. "What's the weather news, Liam?"

"I'll check. It doesn't look good. Maybe we should have turned back home sooner."

Liam made his way back to the cabin now unsteady on his feet as the increasingly turbulent sea buffeted the boat. He reached the galley and sat down a little soaked by the bouncing waves now sweeping overboard. He switched on the ship's radio this time and called the nearest meteorological station 50 kilometres to the north. The weather station answered and he asked for a weather check. It was not good. Hurricane Betsy had not degraded to the extent that had been predicted and its strength had not diminished sufficiently to turn it into a regular storm. This was now developing into a storm-force ten situations and worse. The advice was to get back to port or any safe haven as soon as possible.

Liam made his way back to the bridge and gave John the news. "We'd better get those nets wound back and pronto."

Liam called Billy and Patrick to the back of the boat where two winders with steel ropes on drums were swaying. The increasing strength of the wind made voice communication difficult, but they knew what had to be done. Patrick set the first drum rolling into action hauling the trawl nets back on board, landing on the deck with a smallish catch of silver gleaming wriggling fish.

Billy set the machine to wind in the second trawl net. It moved smoothly at first but was then shuddered to a halt.

"What's wrong?" Liam shouted through the wind.

"Stuck. It's stuck," Billy yelled back.

Liam struggled along the bobbing boat to get to Billy, knowing that nets dangling off the stern could be destabilising and probably perilous in the high stormy seas. It could easily shift the centre gravity of the trawler and with a load of fish on board the effect could be amplified.

They struggled with the drum and cables in the swaying boat for no purpose. It seemed irresolutely jammed.

Chapter 12
East Coast

Bill and Linda Cresswell had inherited their bungalow from Linda's mother back in the 1990s. Happisburgh was not the most picturesque part of the Norfolk coast but they had grown to love it. The house overlooked the sea and they observed the changes in its watery activities from day to day. The calm placid North Sea one day, stretching out to the horizon with the slowly turning propellers of the wind turbines glinting in the sun offering a vision of solid certainty. Then grey wintery days when the sea surges showed a panorama of brooding malevolence. Gusting winds threw up a white spuming surf giving rise to feelings of potential menace. Such things Bill and Linda quickly put to the back of their mind.

"Cup of tea, Bill?"

She heard Bill's faint voice from the bedroom. "Yeah, that'll be lovely, darling."

Linda then heard Bill's familiar coughing and spluttering as she put the kettle on to boil. As she arranged the tea things, she mused. They had been in Happisburgh for what, twenty-five years now. They'd moved in soon after her mother's funeral. She had lived there alone for six years after her father died. Her sister in London was not interested in the property although she occasionally came to visit for, what she pretentiously called a 'staycation'. Linda smiled. You wouldn't believe they were sisters. Her a college lecturer and all. So having no other siblings, she and Bill had decided it would be nice to escape Luton and enjoy a breath of fresh sea air.

At 58, Bill had seized the chance to take redundancy and early retirement from his team leader job at Vauxhall Motors. The prospects had been none too good and now he read from time to time of the gloomy developments of the company's future. He had been right to get out. He had wanted to enjoy a bit of peace and quiet. He missed his old mates but they weren't going to pay his pension or give him a bungalow by the sea. So they had sold up, and like so many others, hoped to live out their twilight years in comfort and peace.

Linda took the tea things into the bedroom where Bill lay propped up on pillows. A small TV was on in the corner with the volume turned down.

"Looks like a storm brewing according to the forecast," Bill said. Linda put the tray down and poured the tea. She sat on the bed and they both looked out the window and observed the growing liveliness of the incoming waves.

"Let's hope it's not a big storm.," Linda said smiling suppressing worrying thoughts.

Bill coughed and sipped his tea. "They say it's the end of that Hurricane Betsy in America. It seems to be heading our way."

"Well, it usually blows itself out before it reaches here and we just get high winds." Linda hoped and prayed that that would be the case.

"Yeah, last year was bad 'un. That storm washed out half the coast and the Jones's back garden disappeared. Just fell in the sea." Bill ruminated on this grim thought.

"Well, let's not get depressed."

"Well, we've got to face facts, love. We are vulnerable according to that bloke from the council who visited last month."

"I'm sure this storm Betty will…"

"Betsy!" Bill corrected.

"Well, anyhow. We don't want to get ourselves down thinking negative thoughts."

"But if it does happen, what will we do?" Bill seemed alarmed. "We can't just stay here and get washed away."

"It won't come to that," Linda snapped.

"All right, girl. Just trying to face facts. What's on the telly then?" He said changing the subject.

He turned the TV volume up.

"And that was the news, and here is Jenny Winthrop with the latest weather."

Linda sighed deeply.

"Hurricane Betsy which has recently devastated the Florida coast and the eastern seaboard of the United States has now moved into the Atlantic Ocean. The hurricane left a trail of devastation and has been registered by US meteorological authorities as the most severe on record. Generally, hurricanes tend to dwindle as they move out into the Atlantic but we do know we will experience the tail end of the storm at least and very windy weather and heavy rain is expected within the next day or two."

Bill switched channels and sighed. "Those poor buggers in America have really gone through the wringer. Hundreds dead and thousands homeless."

"That's one good thing about living in a milder climate," Linda mused.

Chapter 13
A Foreboding

Mark picked up his ringing mobile, looked at the name and number and pressed answer. "Hi, Fiona. How are things?"

"OK. Could be better." Fiona MacDonald was the Chief Environmental Reporter for the *Guardian*.

"Why so?"

"I'm due to cover this incoming storm and my children have unfortunately got the flu. I have to be home with them until they get over the worst. I need someone to dep for me until they're OK again. Could you do that?"

"Sure. No problem. I've been working on related stuff. What's the background?"

"This Storm Betsy's going to be something big. It's got all the hallmarks of disaster written over it. It's lashing the west coast of Ireland and Scotland at the moment as you are well aware, but the speculation is that it will travel around the northern coast of Scotland and head into the North Sea. We need someone to track it from Scotland and get stories and pix. You know local folk grappling with the elements, that kind of thing."

"Do we have a photographer?"

"Yeah. Andy Carpenter. Freelance. He's a good bloke and takes some great pics. I'll send you his contact details after I ring off. I'll contact him as well and give some background and tell him he's on day rates with expenses. I'll try getting background information from here and will send it to you from time to time. You on WhatsApp?"

"Yeah and Facebook, Twitter—the lot."

"Good, we'll use them. OK, I gotta go now the kids need attention. Good luck with the story. I may join you when the kids get better. That's the problem of being a single mother."

Mark rang off and within five minutes, he had the details of Andy Carpenter's email, phone and other information from Fiona. He rang Andy's number which surprisingly did not go to answer the phone.

"Yeah?" A gruff northern voice answered.

"Andy? I'm Mark Rattigan, a friend and colleague of Fiona McDonald. Her kids are ill and…" Andy interrupted.

"Yeah. Just got a text through."

"Are you OK for the assignment?"

"Yeah, of course. I note the storm has already hit Scotland and people are having a grim time there."

"It will travel down the east coast so my best bet would be to go somewhere where it would be quite drastic in its impact."

"Such as?"

"I'll have to look things up. Can I call you in an hour and then we'll arrange to meet?"

"Have you got wellies?" A gruff laugh followed. "I'll await your call."

Mark laughed nervously. "Fine," and rang off.

He then rang Alan Evans commissioning editor for science and the environment.

"Hi, Alan. Mark Rattigan here."

"I'm glad Fiona's contacted you already. I suggested you might take over the story until she's back in harness."

"Good of you. Is it OK to take a cameraman?"

"Well, it can be expensive, who is it?"

"Andy Carpenter. He was recommended by Fiona."

"A good man and a very good photographer."

"We're hoping to get some great pics."

"OK, keep the expenses down and get some good stories and shots. But don't take risks. We don't want you ending up as the main story."

"I'll be careful. I wonder whether you could send me some back stories of places on the east coast of Britain that might be prone to flooding."

"I'll email some back stories to you within the hour."

Mark then went straight online. He hurriedly read through the back stories available and by the time he'd finished, Alan had sent a lot of *Guardian* features. He picked up the phone and rang Andy while reading them on the screen.

"Andy, in the past, it looks like much of the east coast of England and Scotland has borne heavy weather and the main places affected are those with rivers entering the North Sea."

"Such as?"

"Moray Firth, Fraserburgh, Peterhead, Firth of Tay, Firth of Forth."

"That's a lot of ground to cover. Virtually, the whole of the east coast."

"There were heavy rains for the last 12 hours which have swollen rivers and so water is flowing to the coast. With coastal sea surges, that should make a perfect storm. We'll discuss it on the way up to Scotland."

"Scotland?" Andy said in surprise. "I think the storm's already hit Scotland according to the Met Office and working its way down the east coast. I would suggest somewhere in England. We can always get agency stories covering the Scottish angle. I think our best bet is to go to East Anglia."

Mark said hesitantly, "Yeah, you are right. I think we should go by car as we'll need to move around. Where shall I pick you up?"

"Crouch End, OK for you?"

"Give me the address, I'll pick you up in half an hour."

Mark had already packed wet weather gear and was well prepared. He knew the drill. He drove through torrential rain across London. For once, he didn't care about the excess charge and arrived at Andy's place 35 minutes later. Andy was already standing at the front door. He hurried down the steps and threw his bag in the boot but was more careful with his photographic equipment.

"I think we head up the M11 to the A11 turn off and drive to Norwich," Mark said.

Andy gruffly said, "It depends on where you want to go. If you are heading for the coast north of Norwich, then the A12 would be better."

Mark commented dryly, "You sound like my old man. Oooo, I wouldn't go that way you're much better off on the A12."

"Very funny. Just drive."

Mark grinned and thought Andy was gonna be good company. *I hope he has a sense of humour.* The rain continued to fall as they drove up the A12 past Ipswich and on towards Norwich. At Great Yarmouth, they travelled the lesser roads which hugged the coastline. At times, the deluge was so strong the windscreen wipers were finding it hard to cope. They passed through communities which were battered by the rising storm. There were few people about. The houses and bungalows looked forlorn and remote. Rain hurtled down on the roofs and sides of the buildings. Water was running down drains that seemed less and less able to manage the volume. Water spouts and guttering were overflowing and spilling down walls onto the streets. As they drove on, puddles on the road began to grow large and the car splashed through them spraying water to each side.

"I don't like the look of this," Andy said through gritted teeth.

"If we can get to some places between Cromer and Yarmouth, they're the ones most vulnerable."

"Such as?"

"Can you take a look at the map?"

Andy began turning the pages until he located the East Anglia map.

"Well, Happisburgh was mentioned as being one of the most prone places for erosion and…" Mark paused. "Well, let's face the disaster. Some are still sticking it out though."

"Right, Appisburg it is," Andy said fingering the map.

"It's pronounced Haysbrough."

"Well, why don't they spell it like that?" Andy said irritably.

The road was extremely wiggly and they peered out of their windscreen out to the choppy sea which was becoming rougher with each mile they travelled. At last, after a brief turn inland, Happisburgh hove into view. A collection of houses hugged the coastline too near the raging waters for comfort. They were perched on brown cliff tops which seemed no more solid than a pile of compacted dirt. They were later to learn that the cliffs are comprised of clay and sand and extremely prone to erosion, which had been taking place steadily over the centuries. That process had been accelerated by the more frequent and fiercer storms that had been happening in the last 20 years or so.

Although still early evening, vision was limited and although a high wind was blowing the skies were gunmetal grey. It felt like the beginning of a classic gothic horror movie. Beside the end house on the cliff, they noticed lights and a group of people. They seemed very preoccupied and there was a lot of shouting. Mark and Andy climbed out of the car and walked towards the group. A man turned and noticed them and began making his way hurriedly towards them. "You can't come any closer," he shouted through the wind. "This is a danger zone."

"We're reporters covering the storm for a national newspaper. What's happening?"

The man hesitated and then said, "We're trying to get folk out of their houses to safety. Most have gone but there are a few that are stubborn and we're trying to persuade them to leave." Andy already had his cameras out and was taking shots of the houses on the cliff. The wind and rain increased in speed whipping their clothes and stinging their faces. A huge cracking and thunderous noise rent the blustery air. They all turned and looked incredulously. A house was falling off the cliff edge into the raging foam. They rushed towards the space where the house had been. Several elderly people were sobbing and some in tracksuits looked shocked and were uttering, "Oh no, Oh no. We're too late. Bill and Linda are gone."

Mark looked over the cliff edge with the others to see half of a bungalow lying in the lashing seas. A woman close by blinded by anguish and sobbing sunk into the man's arms standing next to her. "Come on, girl, we can't do anything here. Let's get away from here," the man said trying to reassure the grief-stricken woman.

"Who were the people who lived there?" Mark quickly asked not wanting to miss the opportunity.

The man turned to face him. "The Cresswells. Bill and Linda. We tried to warn them but they hung on to the last minute. It was a minute too long."

They turned and walked away with the man's arm around her shoulders comforting the sobbing woman. Andy took pictures of the distressed couple with the cliff tops in the background.

An official-looking man stood nearby and Mark approached him as police and rescue crews hurried down to the nearest beach to see if they could save the couple or salvage the wreckage. It was quite obviously too late. The couple had either been swept out to sea or more likely lay trapped and drowning under the piles of masonry and wood that was once their home. Flashes of electricity occasionally flecked the sky as electrical appliances were wrenched out of their sockets and main cables snapped.

The man turned to Mark and said, "There's nothing we can do for them now. In that sea, we would be lucky to save ourselves let alone rescue anyone. Lord, have mercy on their souls. I did tell them. I tried to tell them to…" The words seemed stuck in his mouth. He stutteringly continued, "I begged them…to leave." The man sobbed. "Sorry. It's been a long day."

"Are you an official?" Mark asked.

"No a volunteer with CCAG."

Mark looked puzzled. "Coastal Concern Action Group. It was formed 25 years ago when it became obvious things were getting worse on the coastal erosion front in these parts."

"So what does it do?"

"Well, not much by the look of it. No, I'm just down really down. My wife and I ran a guest house. That went over the top a few years back just like old Di Wrightson. She had a small hotel cum guest house and a house next to it. Both gone. Just like herself. She's better off out of it. Would you like a coffee or something stronger so we can have a chat away from this nasty weather?"

"Thanks, but I'll need to get a bit more for my article. I'll be down later. Is that OK? Where do you live?"

"That's fine, we ain't going nowhere tonight." He turned and pointed to a road going inland. "See that road? That's Beach Road. We're number 25. Phil McCarty's the name. See you later."

"Yeah, and thanks." Mark and Andy made their way back to the wrecked house now tumbled into the sea. More police and rescue crews had arrived and were planning their next move. Lights were now illuminating the scene and Mark could see that several adjacent buildings looked extremely vulnerable. They chatted to some of the rescue crews who seemed rather pessimistic that they could do much at all except make sure that no more people were in danger and the site was secured.

One of the policemen cynically laughed. "Site secured? There won't be many sites left to secure after tonight I'm sure of that."

"Any news further up the coast?" Mark asked.

"It's bad everywhere. I heard King's Lynn and Hunstanton have considerable flooding. There'll be a lot of homeless people."

Mark watched the rescue teams and Andy took photographs of their activities. Mark finally approached Andy who was crouched down and taking an angled shot. "These waves and stormy seas. Great stuff. Got some really great pix," Andy shouted above the wind.

Mark squatted down beside him. "We'd better get our stories and pix filed," said Mark. "Shall we pay a visit to Phil McCarty? He seemed pretty amenable and, let's hope, charitable."

They walked back to their, drove down the road and found number 25, a white-washed detached cottage set back from the road. It looked snug and cosy in the mayhem of night and a place of shelter. They got out of the car and hurried to the front door. Phil opened the door to them. "Welcome. You look like a couple of drowned rats." Phil showed them into a warm living room and his wife rose from an armchair to greet them.

"This is my wife Jenny." A silver-haired woman who looked younger than Phil came towards them smiling. She held out her hand. "Would you like a cup of tea or coffee?"

"They might like something stronger," Phil said grinning.

"Thanks. Yeah, that'd be good," said Andy immediately.

"I'm OK with coffee," said Mark. "I have to write up a story. Is it OK if we do it here?"

"Be my guest. Do you have anywhere to stay?" Phil enquired.

"Not at the moment."

"Well, you're welcome to stay here. We have a spare room if you don't mind sharing."

"That's very generous of you," Mark said looking at Andy pointedly.

"Yeah, fine. Great. Thanks."

"It would also give me the opportunity to ask you about…what's the name of your community group against the floods?"

"Coastal Concern Action Group or CCAG, for short. Take a seat." Mark could see that now Phil had an interested audience he would let rip about his views. Phil's longish grey hair swished as he quickly sat down, leaning forward to fully capture their attention. His eyes glinted. It was obvious he was going to make the most of this opportunity.

"Well, where shall we start? As I said to you on the cliff top earlier this evening, the action group was started in 1999. We wanted something done about the cliff erosion. It seemed the council and the government were doing precious little. There's been over 25 houses lost over the past 20 years and more are under threat. We were lucky compared to some. We sold our house on the cliff just in time and bought this place farther away from the edge."

Just then Jenny came into the room with a tray which had a bottle of whiskey and two glasses. "I've made you boys some ham and cheese sandwiches. If that's OK?"

"Absolutely fine," Andy said. She put the tray on a small table between them and Phil moved over and poured two whiskeys. "I think I've earned this." He handed a glass to Andy who looked very grateful and at the same time hungrily reached for a sandwich. He then took a generous slug of whiskey. "That hit the spot." Jenny seemed pleased that her hospitality was appreciated.

Mark thanked Jenny and picked up his coffee and a sandwich. He then took out his notebook and looked at Phil expectantly.

"As I was saying, there has been a lot of discontent among people in Happisburgh. Not just here but up and down the coast." Phil paused and took a gulp of whiskey.

"There have been attempts to shore up defences against the sea but nothing that would hold, particularly against the weather we've had in the last few years. We've had politicians, government officials, people from the Environment Agency and North Norfolk Council, but nothing substantial has really been done. They promised back in the 1990s that they'd maintain sea defences. A wall of wood had been constructed and then in 2002, rocks and boulders were put in front of that. It held against your average storm but really has no chance against something like this Hurricane Betsy. One night we lost 10 metres of land. Just fell away and the houses went with it. It'll be more than that tonight I'm sure of that."

Phil took another sip of his whiskey.

"One of the major obstructions to getting proper sea defences is that the government just won't commit to the kind of investment required to save our coastline. As Diana Wrightson said before she died…" Phil paused while he moved to a bureau by the wall and rummaged through some papers. He pulled out an article. "She was one of the driving forces behind CCAG. Yeah, here it is." Phil pulled himself up to his full height as if addressing a meeting. "I quote from this interview she gave to *The New Civil Engineer*." He coughed and read, "The whole system is structured not to spend money. It beggars belief that the government can make decisions that ostracise vast swathes of the country. She was spot on. A bloody good lady was Di."

"Take flooding, for example, back in 2012, Cameron cut a whole load of money from the Environment Agency budget much of which would have gone towards flood defences. They're not interested. This recent lot. Just the same. They've commissioned reports which say that maintaining coastal defences is not, and I quote." Phil straightened up and looked grave 'financially viable'. "That's it then, we're written off. On top of that, insurance companies won't touch us with a barge pole. A lot of people have lost a great deal of money. It's like pouring cash into the sea."

Mark wrote diligently and then looked up. "So what's happening now?"

"We're still trying hard to get the government and other authorities to commit to building local defences. But I think that's becoming a non-runner by the day. They've just given up on us. The other thing we are pursuing trying to get proper compensation. Getting money out of the insurance companies is like getting blood out of a stone. There's more hope there," Phil said glumly belying his last statement.

As Phil seemed to have finished his monologue, Mark asked him if it was OK for them to file their stories. "Yeah, no problem. Jenny will show you up to your room."

"Thanks for the hospitality and the background story. We'll be getting up early tomorrow as we have to follow the storm down the coast."

Jenny got up from her chair. "Don't worry, we get up early. You'll need at least a cup of tea or coffee before you go." Mark then produced a wallet and offered a note. A little 'thank you'.

"No need for that, we're all in this together. I hope you sleep well," said Phil. Mark sheepishly returned the money to his wallet and mumbled a thank you.

At 5 a.m. the next morning, Andy and Mark crept down the stairs but Jenny was already busy in the kitchen.

"Tea or coffee? Would like a bite to eat before you go?" Andy smiled and Mark could see that they would have to eat a hearty breakfast before Jenny would finally let them go. Andy was all in favour.

By the time they had finished their bacon, eggs and toast, Phil had come down. They rose from their seats ready to tackle another day. They thanked their hosts profusely and tried to push some money into their hands which was again politely but firmly rebuffed and having said their goodbyes were on their way. They walked out into the gale. It seemed like it had not let up and they battled their way to the coastal cliffs.

Small groups of police and other officials were talking and attempting to keep out of the worst buffeting of the wind. Some had large mugs of tea in their hands. Mark and Andy approached them and explained who they were and where they had stayed for the night.

"It's been a bad night," a policeman in full weather gear said, "15 houses gone and 20 metres of land."

"Can I get some pictures?" Andy asked.

"There's not much to see but a lot of wreckage. The owners had evacuated long ago."

Andy walked along the coastal path or what was left of it and below lying in the swirling foam were the remains of buildings. Smashed wood, plaster brickwork and concrete were lying on an entirely new shoreline. Debris in the swirling sea was being buffeted onto the sand. Roofs floated out to sea. Front doors which once secured these homes were being washed away towards the horizon, tossed by the still frantic waves. It looked as if a town had vanished. Nothing remained but open fields stretching back to houses further inland.

Andy clicked away while Mark gaped in awe. He was still taking in the impact of the scene.

Chapter 14
The Bump

In the car on the way back to London, Mark had time to think while Andy slept in the passenger seat. Gradually, his thoughts turned to Julie and their marriage. Was it completely over? Could he have one last go in trying to patch it up? If it was over he would miss her and the kids. Yes, he had been thoughtless. He had taken on too many assignments away from home. He had left Julie to cope with, not only the kids and the house but his mother as well. He knew one thing, he still loved her. He still wanted to be with her. But does she feel the same? If it was over, it would be a blow from which he might never fully recover. He would be a lonely ageing hack living…no existing, in his mother's house or at best a studio apartment. Eating takeaways and fast food. Nursing a pint in the pub. No, it was not for him. It would be a grim lonely existence. He knew for sure he had to try his best. It was either Julie or his job, and he was beginning to realise that as much as he loved his job, he loved his wife more.

The wind and rain lashed the side of the car, and then a sudden voice shook him from his reverie. Andy had woken up and put on the radio and was listening to the news. "We must be getting near London, wasn't that Brentwood we just passed?"

"Oh umm. Yeah, you are right," Mark mumbled.

"The news sounds pretty bleak," Andy's northern accent added to the serious nature of the radio voice.

"The extreme weather front brought by Storm Betsy has not abated and is making its way down the east coast to London and beyond. The Met Office is predicting serious consequences as the wind speeds remain high, and the rain has not let up for three days. Flooding of an extreme nature will undoubtedly take place." The announcer's voice was solemnly stern. "Officials and the general public must be on the alert."

"We need to talk to someone with authority and knowledge and then we need to start following the stories."

"Any suggestions?" Andy said rather a bit too cynically for Mark's taste. He decided to ignore it.

"The first port of call would be the Met Office. They have the updates on the storm."

"You won't be needing me then," Andy said curtly.

"We've had a long day and night I think we need a break. Some coffee. There's a Little Chef coming up."

Andy nodded and Mark drove into the roadside cafe.

Mark grabbed his laptop and they both walked wearily inside.

"Sorry, mate. A bit knackered. I'll get these."

"A strong black coffee would be good."

While Andy joined a small queue at the counter, Mark opened his laptop and got the Met Office online. He read with interest. The storm had not abated and was heading towards the mouth of the River Thames and London.

The Met Office also reported the wreckage and carnage in the wake of the storm emphasising its strength. Waves up to 21 metres high had been reported in the Atlantic and the back end of these had hit the west Irish and Scottish coasts hard. Ships were reported lost. Several fishing trawlers had gone down and contact had been lost with others. It was turning into a nightmare of huge proportions.

Andy returned with coffee. Mark gratefully took a gulp. "I think it would be a waste of time going to the Met Office. We need to go somewhere like the Thames Barrier. Get their views and get some pix of water hitting that."

Andy perked up at the suggestion. "Yeah, that would make for some great snaps."

Just then Andy's mobile rang. It was Fiona MacDonald. "How did Norfolk go? Alan sent me a copy of your stories. Great stuff. I'm now freed up as my mother has arrived to look after the kids."

" Why don't you join us we're heading off to the Thames Barrier."

"It looks as if the storm will be doing a great deal of damage to London if the barrier doesn't hold."

"Is that a possibility?" Mark was incredulous.

"It's been talked about for some years. A big storm could breach the barrier. This might be the one."

"We must meet up but where?"

"How about the museum cafe beside the barrier? I could update you on what I've got and we'd be on the scene if anything happens."

"It's 11:15, shall we say noon or as near as damn it. I'll contact you if there are any delays."

"Fine. See you then." Mark and Andy finished their coffees and walked hurriedly out into the wind and rain. It seemed stronger by the minute. The drive to the barrier was relatively trouble-free but finding a parking place proved more difficult and they arrived a little later than anticipated. They climbed the steps to the Barrier Museum cafe and when they entered, it was nearly empty except for a woman in her thirties sitting by the window looking out over the Thames. They made their way towards her. She rose to greet them. "Mark, good to meet you at last," Fiona said. Mark was immediately put at ease by her welcoming smile. She turned to Andy. "Good to see you again, Andy. How are things?"

"The usual." Andy wanted to get the niceties over and get down to business. He looked out over the river to the gleaming edifice of the Thames Barrier. It was impressive. *It was made for great shots,* he thought.

Fiona waved them to a couple of chairs opposite.

"You know about the Bump?" Fiona said. The men stared at her slightly puzzled. "The Bump is a phenomenon long recognised in storm-force conditions. When Hurricane Betsy heads around the north Scottish coast, it hits the North Sea. As the North Sea is much shallower than the Atlantic, it causes the sea to rise giving a bump effect. If that is combined with gale force winds and high spring tides, then the sea can rise even further."

"When you say rise, by how much?" Mark stared at her intently.

"It can be as much as five metres and with this unprecedented storm perhaps more. If that happens, then we're looking at a disaster of gigantic proportions."

"Wow," was Andy's only comment.

Fiona continued, "If that travels down the east coast, as it is now doing, it's going to be catastrophic for London and the low countries. It will overcome most sea defences."

They sat in stunned silence. "This happened in 1953 when Canvey Island was flooded. My father and grandparents were there. It was no picnic then."

"This will be worse," Fiona said emphatically. "Far worse."

Mary, the cafe's manager approached them. "I'm afraid you will have to go now. I've been told to close with this storm coming and everything."

"Can you give me some information about the barrier?" Mark asked in desperation.

"I just run the cafe and we're closing now. Sorry."

"Is there anyone we can speak to? We're journalists tracking the storm and the barrier is a good place to keep up with developments."

"I don't know. You'd have to speak to the Operations Manager Derek Lassiter or one of his staff."

Just then a man walked in. "Hi, Mary. How are things? Have you got a coffee on the go?"

"Speak of the devil. We were just talking about you, Derek."

"Nothing bad I hope," Lassiter glared menacingly.

"Mary mentioned you were in charge. The operations manager," Fiona said smiling.

"So?" Lassiter did not return the smile.

"We're reporters looking for information on the storm and the barrier."

"Look, I'm in an emergency situation here. I haven't got time to…"

"Is it OK if I get your picture for the article?" Andy interjected getting out his camera.

Lassiter's attitude changed immediately. "Article, you say. Well, alright but you'll have to be quick."

"It could be a front-page story," Fiona said buttering Lassiter up further.

"OK, what do you want to know? Five minutes, that's all I'm giving you."

Mark jumped in, "How do you know when to close the barrier? What causes that decision to be made?"

"It's not unusual to close the barrier," said Lassiter as though addressing a class of schoolchildren. "It's been closed 246 times in all. We can get information to do that up to 36 hours in advance. Monitoring stations around the British Isles, the Met Office and the UK National Tideguage Network among other organisations send us regular reports about tides, tidal surges, weather developments etc. This is fed into computers down there," he points through the window to the piers of the barrier.

"We analyse this data and decide whether to take action to close the barrier. We try to do this four hours before peak weather conditions. Once we make that decision, we contact the Port of London Authority and other key personnel." He paused then added as an afterthought.

"Remember the barrier is not just protecting us from the ravages of the North Sea; it also helps control tides of fresh water flowing down the Thames from inland. This is monitored at Teddington Weir. That's where the sea river tide meets the freshwater tide. If there's been heavy rain, like it is now, that can cause heavy flooding in west London and the counties upriver."

"So the barrier controls flows coming in from the North Sea and from inland," said Fiona.

"Do you think it'll be closed now?" Mark asked.

"Highly likely. I've been called in, especially for an extra shift. You only have to look out the window and get the news from the BBC about what's happening in the North Sea at the moment. Also, the Met Office is issuing a red code alert."

"What's that?" Fiona quickly asked.

"OK," said Lassiter testily looking at his watch. "There are three codes yellow, amber and red. The last means dangerous weather is expected. Now I must go." And with that, he picked up his flask of coffee and marched out of the cafe.

They followed him out and sought shelter under an arch. Fiona took control. "Did you get enough, Andy?"

"Too many of that prat, Lassiter. It would be nice to get some of the barriers closing though."

"If the barrier is breached, then we need to contact the emergency services," Mark interjected.

"And that would be?" Andy asked.

"The Port of London Authority to start with and then the emergency services. Police, ambulances, etc," said Mark.

"I think the authorities will deal with that. We need to get some government quotes. They're setting up COBRA," said Fiona.

"What's that?" Andy asked.

"The Cabinet Office Briefing Rooms. It's the committee headed by the prime minister that oversees the emergency with heads of all agencies involved."

"Right," grunted Andy.

"I'll get over to Whitehall and find out what's going on." Fiona slung her bag over her shoulder and was gone.

Chapter 15
COBRA

Fiona emerged from Trafalgar Square station and walked rapidly towards 70, Whitehall, the Cabinet Briefing Rooms or COBRA just behind Downing Street. Fiona approached a gaggle of reporters from newspapers and TV stations who had commandeered the steps leading into the building. "Any developments, Andy?" Andy Jones worked for the *Independent* newspaper and although they knew each other, he didn't want to give too much away to a rival though a sisterly paper.

"Nothing yet," said Andy, "but I'm sure there will be something soon. They've been in there long enough."

"How long?"

"A couple of hours."

Inside the briefing room, Prime Minister Emma Cooper conducted a meeting made of the Department of the Environment, Food and Rural Affairs (DEFRA), The Environmental Agency, London-based police forces, including the Met and Thames Police, the London Mayor's Office, and representatives from some home counties local governments, the Health Services, the armed forces and Rescue Agencies. There was also a specially invited representative from the Meteorological Office.

Emma turned to Jane Olusoga from the Met Office. "How bad is the weather situation right now and could you make it as brief as possible?" Jane turned on her laptop which projected a weather map of the North Sea and British Isles onto a screen behind her.

"Storm Betsy has made its way across the Atlantic and instead of fading as these hurricanes from America normally do, it has remained severe, causing devastation to the west coast of Ireland and Scotland. The storm has rounded the north coast of Scotland and has proceeded into the North Sea and down the east coast of Scotland and England. It has caused considerable damage and injury to many coastal communities."

Emma interrupted. "And now what does this mean for London?"

Anthony Hammond from the Environment Agency interrupted her, "The prognosis is not good. London could well be under threat from a flood the likes of which we have not seen before. We have been in touch with the Port of London Authority who control the Thames Barrier and they are concerned that it might be breached, and that has serious implications for London."

"Yes," continued Jane, "the sea swells making their way down the North Sea coast have grown. We call it the Bump or Hump. Winds have increased the size of the swell and the hurricane although gradually decreasing in power has received an upsurge as a result creating a hump of sea like a large wave. In this scenario, we are looking at something like a small Tsunami."

People looked at each other in the room in alarm. The prime minister grimaced. "What does this mean for London?" Hammond broke in his voice rising to quell the loud murmurs.

"Basically, London is under threat and we should be preparing for the worst. If...no...when that Tsunami comes down the mouth of Thames, it could breach the barrier at Woolwich and head inland to the City of London."

Jane interjected, "In addition, it has been raining for over a week and the home counties are sodden. Many of their run-offs end up in the Thames Valley. So you also have the double whammy of water from inland pouring eastward down the Thames to the North Sea. When these two forces meet, the Tsunami from the east and the river surge and tides from the west the result could only be described as horrendous."

"You mean London will be flooded," Emma stated bluntly.

Jane nodded looking grim.

"That will affect London disastrously without a doubt but in what way?"

"What we know from various commissioned reports is that at least one and a half million people will be directly affected." Hammond looked down and shuffled some papers. He picked up a sheet and began to read. "Over 500,000 homes will be at risk together with 40,000 commercial and industrial properties. 400 schools, 16 hospitals, 8 power stations and more than 1,000 electricity substations."

People turned to each other in disbelief. He continued. "Four world heritage sites will be under threat together with art galleries and historic buildings. On the transport side, 167 kilometres of railway, 35 tube stations, 61 rail stations and over 300 kilometres of road."

"Anything else? That seems pretty comprehensive," the prime minister observed.

"Well, of course, the Houses of Parliament could be flooded as it is directly on the river and much of Whitehall could be underwater."

Chief Commissioner Joseph Charles interjected, "If they are adversely affected then this will pose considerable law and order problems for the police both in terms of guiding people to safety and preventing looting or criminal damage."

"Naturally, the army must have a role in this situation. Moving and herding hundreds of thousands of people will be a mammoth task," said General Pomphrey of the Joint Chief of Staffs.

Jenny Smith from the Department of Health added, "Hospitals like St Thomas's and Guys its sister hospital south of the river, will need patients to be evacuated to places of safety. That's an enormous undertaking in itself."

The London Mayor intervened, "Of course, the transport system will be in chaos with many tube stations flooded and together with overland services the system of transport will be in disarray. People will be trying to leave work and people from affected homes will be attempting to flee the situation."

"What plans do we have to deal with this situation, Mr Hammond?"

"The Environment Agency has drawn up several plans with concerned agencies most of whom are represented around this table."

"In June 2014, we published a mass evacuation framework under what was then called The London Resilience Partnership."

"We haven't got time for a detailed analysis. Could you summarise as quickly as possible its main findings please?" Emma Cooper looked stern. "I'm eager to get this meeting over and for these agencies to do their work."

"OK, in the event of catastrophes to the city, we have developed two responses with our partners under a mass evacuation framework. These are under the headings 'sudden impact incident' and 'rising tide incident'. There will be considerable overlap between the two."

"Can you keep it brief and to the point? We are in an emergency situation, Mr Hammond," Emma interjected aware of the ponderous detail into which civil servants can sometimes get lost.

"Ah yes, in a nutshell, there are evacuation procedures categorised as the following. One, those who can self-evacuate i.e., flee the situation under their own steam. Two, those who will need assisted evacuation i.e., people capable of transporting themselves but will need support in terms of directions towards safe places. Thirdly, those that need full support i.e., the vulnerable."

"And how effective will these arrangements be?" Emma cut in.

"They have never been fully tried for obvious reasons."

"How will we keep the population informed?"

"Through the usual channels and some social media networks. We have asked London residents to sign up to our emergency scheme but that has only been taken up by a small number of people. Local councils should have set up communication channels through local radio and TV and also distribution of leaflets, but the last one is now a little late."

"And what about resources?" Emma stared around the room for someone from the Treasury.

Anthony Hammond stuttering quickly interrupted, "Err...I know this may sound controversial and political but resources for emergency situations have been pared down to the minimum. The austerity measures between 2010 and 2020 followed by the emergency measures to deal with the Covid-19 crisis, and, as you know, Prime Minister, followed by further cutbacks in the public sector to deal with the recession of 2022 to 2024 which means resources have been considerably depleted."

Alarmed chattering broke out around the room. He continued, "However, we did learn some valuable lessons in dealing with the Coronavirus epidemic."

"Such as?" The prime minister pointedly said.

"Umm, well to have a strategy and plan and to stick to it."

The prime minister spoke loudly and sternly. "We seem to have a strategy and a plan and we must do the best we can. Please, attend to your duties. This meeting has ended. We will reconvene tomorrow first thing in the morning." With that, she picked up her papers and strode from the room.

Outside Fiona and the rest of the media reporters sprang into action as the prime minister descended the steps to her official car. A cacophony of questions erupted from the reporters.

"Prime Minister, what's being done to avoid the storm?"

"Prime Minister, what are doing to avert total disaster to the capital?"

As the cameras rolled and bulbs flashed, she turned and said calmly. "We will do everything possible. All government resources are now fully concentrated on dealing with the situation. Thank you." She then climbed into a waiting limousine which drove round the corner to Downing Street.

As the rest of the COBRA members began leaving, reporters pounced on them hoping for some solid information. Most hurried through the clutch of media journalists. A cabinet office spokesperson waited on the higher steps and announced, "The Prime minister will be making a detailed statement in one hour when we have a clearer picture of the weather situation." Reporters rushed to him as he attempted to take the short walk around the corner to number 10.

Fiona spotted a civil servant she knew who had fed her off-the-record information in the past. "James, how are you?"

James looked around alarmed and realising it was Fiona stopped briefly and said, "Walk with me." They left the throng with Fiona traipsing behind him. As they rounded a corner, James turned and said, "Off the record?" Fiona nodded vigorously. "OK, you can use this but my name doesn't come into it. Understand?"

"Of course, you'll be 'a reliable anonymous source'."

"Good." He looked tense and grim. "It's a disaster. This'll make Covid-19 look like a picnic."

Chapter 16
Oikos Canvey Island

Kevin Manwaring drove his car up to the Oikos Storage facility. The remotely controlled gates opened as he approached. "Filthy day," he mumbled to himself as he drove through. As senior manager, he felt an obligation to be on duty. He had heard the weather forecasts and they sent an uneasy feeling through him. He was well aware that storms particularly this Betsy could place the Canvey Island facility in a challenging position, particularly as he had heard that it was going to be a monster.

He had related to himself many times to the catastrophe of the Canvey flood of 1953. It was a scenario he did not want to experience himself. Not today or anytime. He reassured himself that proper flood measures and procedures were now in place; after all, this was 2026, what could go wrong?

He parked, jumped out of the car pulling his coat collar up as he hurried to the main entrance, with the rain soaking him and the wind tugging at his clothes. Through the door, he stopped and brushed off the raindrops. "Dreadful weather, Miranda," he called to the woman on the main desk.

"Yes, Mr Manwaring, looks like we're in for a rough one." Manwaring hurried upstairs to his office sliding off his wet coat on the way.

He walked along the corridor to a door marked Bob Lewington's Shift Supervisor. He knocked and entered. "Hi, Bob. How are things?"

"Nasty storm brewing. I think we need to close down after this tanker has unloaded."

"Is that the one on Jetty 2?"

"Yeah, the 'Ocean Queen'. Just in from Rotterdam."

"She's big, but nothing our newly revitalised jetty can't handle." Kevin was proud of the updated and refurbished jettys which could now take ships of up to 122,000 tonnes. It had also been extended out to deeper waters with a length of

277 metres. Sixty metres longer than the old jetty which lay a few hundred yards away. In addition, most of the 38 container tanks on shore had been upgraded and refurbished. The facility was reckoned to be one of the safest in an industry which has had its ups and downs with some bad accidents in the past.

"How much more has she got to make the final drain?"

"I'll ask Jimmy." He picked up a walkie-talkie talkie and static filled the office momentarily. Jimmy West was one of the shift operators. He picked up immediately. "The Ocean Queen. How long has she got?"

"Hi, Bob. She's a big one. I reckon another hour maybe an hour and a half."

"This storm's coming in pretty fast, can we hurry up, Jim?"

"I'm doing my best. It's bloody wet and windy down here. The captain isn't looking too pleased either."

"What's his name?"

"Captain De Brunner. He's anxious to finish as quickly as possible as well."

"Ah, De Brunner. Not the easiest man to deal with. Well, do the best you can, Jimmy."

"Righto, Bob." He turned to Kevin. "It'll be another hour maybe an hour and a half."

"It's just a waiting game then."

Kevin picked up a leaflet from Bob's desk. "What's this?"

"It's from Canvey Green Belt Campaign. They're bellyaching about cuts in the Essex Fire and Rescue services and not being consulted. More worryingly, they've dragged up health and safety issues about us concerning the storage plant."

"What?" Kevin seemed incredulous. "We have the best health and safety arrangement bar anyone anywhere in the world."

"They've also dragged up the Calor gas leak which occurred on Canvey back in 2010. They state…if I may?" Bob took the leaflet out of Kevin's hands and read, "It was by good fortune that the gas leak did not find a source of ignition. They're also constantly referring to the Buncefield Disaster of 2005."

Kevin cut in, "That was a disaster. Caused by neglect and poor monitoring. One of their storage tanks overflowed in the filling process. The capacity gauge malfunctioned and fluid spilt out which quickly turned to highly flammable gas and exploded taking 22 tanks with it."

"Yeah, I know. It ruined quite a number of residential homes nearby and the blast could be heard in France and Belgium! Fortunately, there were no fatalities."

"Do they think another Buncefield could happen here? We went through all that stuff in our H&S review and have made sure that can't happen here."

"Well, they're worried about the expansion of the site and the possible hazards."

"Umm," Kevin grunted and then looked as though he had forgotten something.

"I'll tell Miranda she can go home. There's nothing for her to do here. I'll also check how the pumping's going." Kevin returned to his office and phoned the reception desk.

A moment later, Bob entered Kevin's office with some papers. "I have the offloading documents here."

Kevin read them. "I see the loading master has checked through everything with Chief Officer De Brunning. It all looks good."

"That storm's getting pretty close; I have a good mind to give the emergency order to stop the pumping. It's a race between getting the fuel ashore and the arrival of the storm. Those pipe connections between ship and shore could be at risk."

He put the papers down on the desk. "What do you think, Bob?" He looked up at a rather concerned face. Bob seemed unable to say anything.

"I think we can risk it," Kevin finally said. "Keep the pumping going."

Chapter 17
Tilbury Docks

18 miles along the north shore of the Thames from Canvey Island lies Tilbury Docks, the principal port of London owned by Forth Ports.

Bill Barrington, the CEO of Tilbury Docks guided two men in suits into his office. David Sims, Health and Safety Inspector from the Ministry of Environment, and Richard Scott, a representative from the Port of London Authority, who had jurisdiction over the care of the large facility. It was a good size room with a large desk at one end and at the other a large pine table with six chairs. They shuffled through the door. He threw out his arm. "Please, take a chair, gentlemen. Would you like some coffee or tea?" Bill was a tall burley man with a friendly outgoing personality. Although affable, he could be serious and ultimately tough if the occasion demanded. Today he was at his diplomatic best.

David Sims pulled out a chair and sat down at the long pine table. "Thanks, Bill. Tea will be fine." He took out some papers from his briefcase headed Environment Agency and placed them in front of him. Richard Scott sat down beside him. "Coffee, thanks, Bill." He placed a blank writing pad in front of him. He looked at the large picture windows now covered in rain as the storm outside increased in ferocity.

Bill picked up the phone. "Grace, could you bring in a couple of coffees and a tea, please?" He looked at the two men. He put the phone down and sat at the end of the table in what was obviously taken to be the chairman's place.

Bill opened the meeting. "I hope we've made you comfortable in the past two days while you have been inspecting the facilities. As you have seen for yourselves, it covers a large area; a hundred acres with 10 kilometres of quayside."

"I can understand why it is one of the major ports in the UK," said David Sims. "There's a lot to monitor and manage out there," he said looking towards one of the rain-flecked windows.

"Yeah. Nice to be in the dry. Looks like a biggie blowing up out there." Richard nodded in agreement. Bill and Richard often had dealings with each other and were familiar with each other's modus operandi in meetings. The Port of London Authority was continually checking and tracking ship movements which plied the river, and this often gave the two men cause to communicate and sometimes meet to exchange new developments and information.

David Sims turned one of the pages over in front of him. "This is a major container port and import centre for grain. It has 200 separate silos and approximately 2 million tonnes of grain per year are handled here. It also has two paper terminals and holds at one time 2 million tons of recycled products including recycled woodchips. It is also the nearest cruise ship terminal for London."

"That's about right," said Bill. "A hell of a lot to cover and I think we do it pretty well."

"In the normal run of things," said David.

Bill was about to ask what 'normal run of things' meant—he didn't like the sound of that, but they were interrupted by the arrival of the tea and coffee.

Tensions mounted as Grace placed the tray of drinks, milk and sugar on the table and left the room. Bill rose taking the opportunity to calm himself down. He poured the two teas and then the coffee. "Milk?" They both nodded. "Sugar?" Both shook their heads.

"Didn't you have a fire in a wood chip pile in 2018 and 1,500 tonnes were alight?" David Sims looked serious. "And it's noted here that there was a fire in a dust extractor in 2019."

"That's all been checked and dealt with and we monitor that more carefully now. Richard would agree." He turned to look at Richard who nodded.

David Sims continued, "Then in 2023, you had a fire again in one of the paper terminals."

Bill immediately replied, "That was caused by one of our employees who contravened the health and safety rules by smoking in the terminal. The man fully admitted to it and was subsequently dismissed. We then had larger signs put up about not smoking and the group leader was told to make more regular checks and reinforce the no smoking message and the dangers of fires. Since then, there have been no incidents."

"Yes, we noted that," said Richard. David turned over another paper.

"Then last year, one of the containers was dropped from a crane. The investigation showed undue speed to be the principal cause."

Before he could carry on, Bill intervened, "Yes, the investigation revealed human error as the cause."

"What happened to the man?"

"His team leader interviewed him, with myself present. The man had worked in Tilbury for 12 years and never had a blemish on his record. We gave him a thorough interview during which he admitted he had been overly hasty as he had wanted to finish early. He was contrite, admitted his error and promised not to do it again. Given his long and good record and being an experienced operator, we decided to give him another chance. The other operators were also brought into the process and extra training was organised for all teams. There has been no reoccurrence of this kind of incident."

"I'm glad to hear it. I know you are aware that there are a lot of materials stored here that are a potential fire hazard and must be carefully checked. You are experienced and responsible but in the daily run of things sometimes these things get overlooked and before you know it there's a major disaster."

Bill didn't like being talked to as if he were a junior trainee but bit his tongue and nodded.

"Richard and I have now had a thorough inspection of the site and we agree that it is now considered a safe site."

"Good." Bill looked relieved.

"Given the appalling weather, I think Richard and I will take our leave. A full report should reach you within a week." With that, David shuffled his papers and returned them to his briefcase. As he stood up, Bill crossed the room put out his hand and shook David's hand vigorously relieved that they had a clean bill of health. Richard also rose and shook his hand. "I've heard a nasty storm is blowing this way. That will certainly test your facilities." It was meant as a joke but all three men suddenly realised the import of the comment. They hurriedly left. Bill crossed the room and looked out of the window.

As soon as they had left, he went into his secretary's reception area. "Grace, it doesn't look good out there, I think you ought to go early."

"Thank you, Mr Barrington, that's very good of you."

Bill returned to his office. The Thames was wild and choppy with squalls buffeting the few boats smaller than ocean-going liners that dared venture out.

Chapter 18
Dartford Crossing

Jack Rollins sat in his lorry listening to LBC radio. He gazed down the line of traffic on the Dartford Crossing Bridge in front of him. The vehicle swayed slightly in the increasing wind. The coverings of some trucks ahead flapped at their sides. There had been some hold-up. It looked like a broken-down truck half a mile ahead. Traffic was slowly moving out to overtake it. On the radio, the music stopped and a voice said, "We interrupt this music for a weather warning. A storm of increasing intensity is approaching London and the government is advising people to return to their homes as soon as possible."

Jack gazed out the front of his cab. *Bloody well, hurry up!* He thought *I'd like to get home too.* Jack had just made a delivery of goods to Lakeside Shopping Centre in Thurrock and was now heading south across the River Thames to Blue Water at Greenhithe near Dartford. It was his last delivery of the day and after this, he could go home. *The quicker the better*, he thought looking out the side window at the increasingly rough water of the Thames winding away to the east blasted by squalls and gusts of wind.

Eventually, in the distance, he noted a man near the broken-down truck waving traffic past. *At last! I must have lost at least half an hour*, he thought. After some minutes, the lorry in front began moving and he allowed his vehicle to roll slowly forward too. Five minutes later, he passed the now abandoned vehicle and a police officer directing the flow.

Within twenty minutes, he was driving into the Blue Water complex. He parked his vehicle and found it difficult to close the door as blasts of wind and rain buffeted him. He quickly walked into the loading bays of Marks and Spencer and knocked on the office door of the store manager's office.

Both of these large shopping complexes were close to the river and attracted thousands of people to their retail outlets, cinemas and landscaped park areas.

Chapter 19
Teddington Lock (1)

In the main hall of Stanley Primary School, children sat in rows chattering. As the Head Teacher, Carla Meredith, entered the hall with a visitor, the children looked up and the din subsided.

Carla Meredith held out her arms and lowered them down in a gesture for hush. Soon the buzz of talking children ceased.

"Good morning, children."

The children replied in a collective chant.

"Good morning, Mrs Meredith."

"Today we have a special visitor Julia Standish who is the Lead Lock and Weir Keeper at Teddington Lock. As the River Thames is quite close to us, she will explain to you about the river and the fascinating series of locks and weir at Teddington."

Carla stepped to one side to allow Julia to be seen. Behind her on a wall was a large screen with the title 'Teddington Locks' and her name and title.

"Good morning, children. I am very pleased to be here to tell you about the Locks and Weir at Teddington, but I hope you can join in the talk as well. If you have a question or answer, you would like to give, please put your hand up."

She pressed the remote button and a large picture of the Thames at Teddington Locks appeared.

"Does anyone know what a lock is?"

A number of hands rose immediately. Some shouted, "Miss, Miss."

Julia said, "I only answer those with their hand up not those who call out."

She pointed to a little a little boy of Asian origin in the middle row.

"It's what lets you go uphill and downhill by boat," he said enthusiastically.

"Well done! That's exactly it. It's a clever device to allow a boat to go up and down different levels on a river. At Teddington, we have three types of lock to do that." Julia then pressed the remote and a picture of the locks appeared.

"There's a lock for barges, one for river launches and one for skiffs and small boats." She changed the picture to one showing skiffs. "Skiffs would be buffeted or indeed turned over if it shared a lock with a large boat like a barge." A picture of a barge came on the screen. "Even a launch, which is bigger than a skiff, but smaller and lighter than a barge, could get knocked around; so different types of boats sharing the same lock could be dangerous. That's why we have three locks."

Julia then continued to explain how the locks worked. "Now we know how locks work, what is a weir and what is it for? Does anyone know?"

Once again hands shot up around the hall. She pointed to a girl with ginger hair and freckles in the second row.

"Is it to control the river, miss?"

"And how does it do that?"

"By gates that open and shut?" The girl said uncertainly.

"Well done again. But why do we have to control the river?"

Looks of puzzlement crossed a number of the children's faces causing them to look at the person sitting next to them as if they knew the answer.

A girl sitting at the back with dark curly hair slowly raised her hand.

"Is it about tides and the rising of the water?" She spoke with some uncertainty.

"What a clever lot you are," said Julia turning to Carla and smiling.

"Yes, it's partly about tides."

She pushed back her long blond hair from her face and pressed the remote control again. A map appeared.

"This is the River Thames and as you can see it flows from inland eventually out to the sea. The mouth of the Thames eventually emerges in the North Sea. But there is only a tide up to Teddington Lock. The tide means the water can rise, depending on the time of year, by up to 7 metres. That's as high as this hall." All the children looked up and some gasped.

"It can also fall as well. It does this twice a day." Julia paused and said, "Why would the water be salty up to Teddington Lock?"

A few hands shot up but many looked baffled.

"Why do you think it's salty?" Pointing at a tall black boy at the back.

"Cos it is seawater, miss."

"You are a clever bunch. So why would there be freshwater beyond Teddington Lock?" She indicated with the red light pen the upper reaches of the Thames.

A few hands were raised. "Yes," she pointed to an Asian girl at the front.

"Is it because the water doesn't come from the sea, but from land upriver."

"Yes, it does. When it rains, water runs off the hills and into the rivers and the Thames has a lot of rainwater, especially in wet weather."

She once again changed the picture on the screen which now showed a torrent of water.

"If there is a lot of rain, it can overwhelm the river and when that happens, there are lots of floods in many parts of the upper reaches of the Thames."

Another picture came on the screen showing floods. Fields and roads were covered in water with abandoned cars. The children gasped.

"Yes, it can be quite nasty and dangerous. The weir tries to control these upsurges of water by closing gates and preventing too much water from coming downstream, but sometimes in very bad stormy weather, there is so much rain that it can overwhelm the locks and the weir and then the water flows into the tidal part of the Thames. When that happens, you can get flooding in the tidal river." The red pointer indicated a stretch of water beyond Teddington.

"We have had bad flooding in the past at Hammersmith, Ealing and Richmond and other parts of the river. But it could get worse." She leaned forward to emphasise this. The children looked goggle-eyed.

"If there is a bad storm that causes a surge of water to come up the Thames from the estuary like a big wave…"

She again used the red pointer pen to indicate the mouth of the Thames. "And if there was a big flood coming down the Thames because there had been a lot of rain, what do you think might happen?"

She looked around the hall at the children whose imaginations were working overtime in an effort to absorb the information and the question.

A girl in the front row put her hand up hesitantly. "Would there be a huge crash, miss, of the water coming down and the water coming up?"

"Yes, precisely. It would create enormous flooding in those areas near the river and beyond." She paused. "So far that has not happened, but if we get a big storm in the North Sea and a lot of rain coming down the hills of the Thames

Valley, like today…" She paused again. Some children looked alarmed. "Then it could happen."

She turned towards the screen and changed the picture to a group of people. Some were wearing life jackets.

"That's why we need trained people to look after Teddington Lock. It's a very important point on the Thames. We have five full-time lock and weir keepers at Teddington, including three women, and in normal times, they would operate all day and all night in shifts. Any incident—a police incident, pollution, and many other things are dealt with by us, the police and emergency services."

A boy put his hand up eagerly. Julia indicated for him to speak. "What kind of police incidents are there, miss?"

"It can be many things," said Julia un-phased by the question. "People in difficulties swimming or boating, and that happens more than most people think. It could be theft. Sometimes boats are stolen and there are even drowned people." There was a collective intake of breath by the children.

"But our main job concerns the river levels. Alarms go off if water levels drop too low or rise too high, we then adjust the levels by using the gates on the weir. There are 18 gates at Teddington Weir and each is able to be adjusted individually, sometimes at 3 o'clock in the morning if needed."

While Julia was explaining the process, a woman entered the hall with a piece of paper in her hand and walked quietly over to Carla Meredith and whispered in her ear. Carla read the piece of paper and approached Julia who turned to her smiling.

"Excuse me, children, for a moment."

Carla talked quietly to Julia who read the paper. She then turned to the children and said, "I am very sorry but we have an emergency at the Lock and I must go. But thank you for being an attentive and intelligent audience. Let's hope I can finish the talk another time." And with that, she hurriedly left the hall taking her mobile phone out of her pocket.

Chapter 20
Belmarsh Prison

Governor Rosslyn Lee looked at the laptop on his desk and picked up the phone. His secretary answered. "Mary, can you get me Chief PO Marshall as quickly as possible please?"

"Yes, Mr Lee."

She picked up a wireless walkie-talkie and paged Chief PO Marshall.

Marshall responded to the beep on his device and clicked the talk button.

"Yes, what is it?"

"Mary here. The governor wants you in his office immediately."

Brian Marshall was a little annoyed. No please but a blunt order. He hurried through the Belmarsh Prison security system with POs unlocking and locking doors for him as he went.

He arrived outside the governor's office and Mary waved him in.

"Sorry to have called you so abruptly, Brian, but I have been in contact with the Home Office and they are saying due to the severity of the storm, we are going to have to evacuate the prison. I have ordered a large chopper for the high-security category prisoners and vehicles with armed guards will be arriving to transport the rest. We have a plan for evacuation as you know but we want that plan to work perfectly."

"Will it be that bad, Sir?"

"I thought that myself and questioned the Home Office bod. His reply was quite startling. He said that the Thames Barrier could well be breached. As you know, we have had flooding before in Thamesmead but not on this scale. We must make sure that the evacuation of all the prisoners is smooth and trouble-free, especially the high category which contains inmates convicted of terrorist offences."

"I'll get on to it immediately, Sir."

"The vehicles will be arriving within 30 to 40 minutes and the chopper any time soon. As you know, Brian, we have some dangerous inmates who would love to seize the opportunity to escape or at least cause trouble, so we must not tell the prisoners anything until they are ready to be shipped out."

"It's not going to be easy, Sir. Some of these guys are pretty angry and we are short-staffed."

"You don't have to tell me, Brian, I've been badgering the Home Office for the past 10 years along with all the other prisoner governors in Britain."

He hesitated then suddenly looked straight at Brian as if realising the seriousness of the situation. "Well, there's no time for a political debate. Let's get this evacuation done."

"One more question, Sir. Where are the prisoners to be evacuated to?"

"The high-security prisoners are to be separated and to go to category A prisons. The rest will be put where there is space. Even open prisons. A list has already been distributed." He took up a piece of paper from his desk and handed it to Brian.

"Here's a list of the designated prisons for non-high-category prisoners. The chopper crew has orders to take the high-category prisoners to three top-security prisons."

Ten minutes later, the governor and CPO Marshall were overlooking the disgorgement of prisoners from the main block. Many were looking puzzled. "What's going on then? What's all the fuss about, and why are we moving out?"

A hardened thickly built prisoner officer replied, "Never you mind, Rawson. You just keep calm and everything will be OK."

Chapter 21
Silvertown

20 miles eastward along the north shore of the Thames at the Tate and Lyle factory at Silvertown, the day shift was coming to an end and the skeleton night shift was taking over. A large ship lay docked at the wharf near the factory unloading a consignment of raw sugar from the Caribbean. Some of the night shift workers had been given duties overseeing the sugar being unloaded and transported to the factory a few hundred yards away.

Gary Gale turned to his partner Winston Clark. "Cigarette?"

"You should give that up especially working in such a place with flammable stuff all around us."

"Ah, no harm, Winston, we're outside anyway." He took a puff on his cigarette and they watched the ship being unloaded by a huge dredger which dug deep into the hold and pulled up a large bucket load of raw sugar. They watched as the crane turned and placed the load on a conveyor belt which ran into the main factory. There it would be processed into pure sugar and other products. Winston pulled up his collar and hugged his coat closer to him.

"I hope we get finished before this storm comes. It's blowing nigh on a gale." Winston's Caribbean accent gave the warning an archaic sense of profundity, as though they were mid-Atlantic waiting for a pirate invasion.

"Well, I'm Gale by name and it looks as though I will be experiencing my name first-hand." They both laughed and Gary took a long puff on his cigarette the smoke speeding away from his mouth in the blustery wind.

They looked at the ship which was beginning to rock gently in the increasingly choppy waters.

"It looks as though we're in for a dodgy shift weather-wise." Gary threw down his half-smoked cigarette and stamped his foot on it.

"The sooner we get this lot unloaded, the better." Winston gazed out across the increasingly turbulent Thames. He hid his anxieties with a philosophical expression and an attempt at humour. "There must be enough sugar here to rot the teeth and create diabetes in the whole British population." Gary laughed obligingly but grimly.

Chapter 22
St Thomas Hospital

Joe Bacon sat in his car at the hospital drop-off and collection point. Squalls of wind drove rain into the windscreen. He turned to the elderly man beside him. "Dad, it's the best place for you. It'll only be a small operation. You'll soon be out and I'll come and pick you up in no time."

"Mm. Once you go into these places, you never come out." The old man's grumpiness hid his anxieties.

"It's not Victorian times, Dad. These are the best people in the country. Probably the world."

"I still don't like it."

"Well, I can't stay here for any length of time. This is only a drop-off point. Let's get you into reception."

Joe got out of the car walked around to the passenger side and opened the back door and got out a walking stick. He then opened the passenger door and helped his father out. They walked hesitantly and slowly to the main door and reception desk.

"Can I help you?" The smiling receptionist said. "Yes. My father has an appointment for an operation."

"Could you give me his name, please?"

"James Bacon." She tapped his name into the computer. Then turned and smiled again.

"It's for a knee replacement surgery," Joe said trying his best to enlighten the receptionist.

"Oh yes, a knee arthroplasty. He has a bed in Esther Ward in the Orthopaedics Department. I'll just phone for a nurse to come down for you. While you are waiting, could you fill in this form please?"

"I can't stop long as I have my car still at the drop-off point outside."

"Don't worry about that. We'll have dealt with Mr Bacon in a few minutes."

He filled in the form and handed it over. Just then a nurse appeared with a wheelchair.

"Mr James Bacon?"

He looked up.

Joe turned, "Yes, that's my father."

"Jim, not James. I never liked James. Too posh," said his father petulantly. The nurse and Joe helped him into the wheelchair.

"I'm Nurse Anita Gupta, Jim," she said pointedly smiling down at Joe's father.

"Here's his pyjamas, dressing gown and other clothes and err...washbag," said Joe hesitantly handing them over to the nurse. He was feeling distinctly uncomfortable leaving his father so soon.

"Don't worry, Mr Bacon, we'll look after him. We have a nice ward overlooking the Thames. He'll like that."

Joe gave a concerned smile and then patted his father on the back. "See I told you you'd be fine."

"Right, James," said the nurse, turning the wheelchair around.

"Jim. It's Jim."

"Sorry. Of course, Jim," said the nurse.

"Be good now," said Joe pathetically as he watched his father wheeled off down the corridor. "I'll see you tomorrow." There was no reply from his dad. This only made him feel even more guilty.

"He'll be fine with Anita, she's lovely," said the receptionist reassuringly.

Joe smiled nervously and nodded. He then walked out into the rain and wind. It seemed as though the weather had got worse since he had been inside.

An official-looking man approached him. "Is that your car, Sir?"

"I'm just going. I've been dropping off my dad. He can't walk very well."

"That's alright, Sir, but this is a restricted parking zone and we don't like people to hang around too long."

"I understand. I shall be visiting my dad tomorrow and I shall come on foot."

"I think that's for the best, Sir."

Joe hurried out to his car and was grateful to climb in, out of the rain.

Chapter 23
COBRA Two

Prime Minister Emma Cooper stood up to address the pared-down COBRA Committee.

"We now know the situation regarding the storm is putting the east coast of Britain under great strain and the rescue services deployed along the coast are valiantly dealing with a difficult if not impossible situation. It seems almost certain that London is in similar danger and that is why this committee will now meet permanently to coordinate activities until the crisis is over. We need to act quickly and decisively and that is why this has been pared down in membership comprising only essential services, the Mayor of London and representatives from the Ministry of the Environment. This allows for quicker consultation and coordination of actions." Emma cast her eyes around the room. "You will then convey our orders to your networks."

The group members nodded their approval. "What have the public been told?"

Anthony Hammond from the Ministry of the Environment rose to speak.

"All radio, television stations and social media platforms with an official presence are spreading the word that the impending storm may have potentially hazardous consequences for the capital. People are being urged not to travel on the tube or overground railways near the Thames. Many of these services were to be halted in any case. Similarly, people were warned that buses and transport were not to be used which crossed the river or ran close to it."

"What about evacuation plans?" Emma interrupted.

"The evacuation of potentially affected areas has been ordered and is now being carried out."

"Has the Thames Barrier been raised?" Emma stared at Hammond intently. "Can anything be done to contain the effects of the coming storm?"

"The Port of London Authority informs me that the barrier is being raised as we speak and should be fully closed by now. In addition, all sluice gates along the Thames into the city have been closed."

"Good. Let's hope it is enough," said Emma. Nobody spoke. It was a silent acceptance that it probably wouldn't be.

Hammond continued, "The monitoring stations at Southend and Sheerness on either side of the Thames estuary report a very high tide. The storm surge has now combined with the Thames high tide and..." Hammond tailed off as the prime minister interrupted.

"What does that mean exactly?" She said sharply.

"It means that the Thames barrier will probably be unable to hold the water back coming down the river towards London and the city." There was a deathly silence in the room.

Hammond continued, "That's not all, Prime Minister." Emma stared at him intently as if to say there's more.

He coughed. "Water will also be coming down the Thames from the east. As you know it has been raining intently for the past week and a half and this means a considerable amount of water will be coming off the hills surrounding the Thames Valley. In the past, this has resulted in considerable flooding on either side of Teddington Weir, where the Thames North Sea tide meets the upper reaches tide."

"Which areas will be affected?" Emma interjected.

"As I said in the past, places like Hammersmith, Acton and Ealing have been badly flooded."

"Have these places been alerted?"

"Yes, Prime Minister. All those areas are now being warned and housing and businesses close to the river have been warned that the Thames embankments are likely to be breached."

"What about bridges and tall buildings?"

"They are unlikely to be affected in the sense of them falling down. Places like Canary Wharf, for example, may be flooded in the basement areas and its train station but the upper parts of the building are very unlikely to be affected as the building structure is solid and can withstand most adverse conditions. It would take a nuclear explosion to fell a building of that size."

"Right, let's take a break and meet back here in 15 minutes unless anything happens immediately." With that, Emma rose from her chair and walked from the room. A small group of security staff and advisors followed her.

Chapter 24
Estuary

Where the Thames reaches the North Sea, the estuary is 10 miles wide. It is full of sandbanks and shoals and can be treacherous to the unknowing person. The water changes from shallows and sand banks at low tide, where islands of sand can lure on the unwary traveller, to deeper cross-current swirls at high tide. At times of clement weather, its calm surfaces hide this potential maelstrom. Bad weather and heavy storms reveal the dangers of the higher seas.

Hurricane Betsy now a little degraded but potentially threatening had rounded Ireland and the north coast of Scotland. It had wreaked its devastation down the eastern coast communities of Scotland and England wrecking houses, flooding villages and towns and it had finally reached the mouth of the Thames. The main front of the storm would travel on to the low countries where its power would overwhelm the defences of Holland and Belgium built up over the years. The promise of the dire effects of global warming was now unfolding in the usually safer waters of the North Sea, and now it was about to travel down the Thames itself.

At the Oikos Oil Refinery depot, Jim continued to oversee the pumping of the oil from the tanker 'Ocean Queen' to the shore storage tanks. He looked anxiously at the sky. The wind was now strong and he could see high waves looming out on the estuary.

This is no ordinary storm, he thought.

Suddenly Captain de Brunner was at his side. "I think you ought to stop the procedure, it's getting very dangerous. Look at that sea out there."

"I've been instructed to carry on."

"Well, I'm telling you to stop. I am the captain of this tanker and I override your boss." De Brunner was red-faced and angry-looking. "This will put all our lives at risk not to mention the boat."

Just as he said 'boat', a large wave buffeted the ship and the oil nozzle connected to the shore and the boat began to writhe uncontrollably. Jim needed no more cajoling. He was now uncoupling the pipe connections as fast as he could. Just as he had undone the last pipe, a huge wave knocked him and de Brunner off their feet. Oil began to spill out of the hoses and onto the decks, then the landing stages and into the sea.

Cables on land swung wildly in the wind and sparks flew off the connecting ends. An old oil derrick swayed dangerously in the wind. There was a sudden crash as the derrick finally collapsed bringing the cables down too. Flailing ends began to thrash around finally touching some of the spilt oil from the tanker. A huge flame burst into the sky and the fire quickly began to work its way along the spillage towards the ship. Within minutes, flames were beginning to engulf the bobbing tanker. Fireballs of ignited gases leapt into the air. Jim, De Brunner and other men working on the benighted vessel didn't stand a chance. The flames rose in the air in a huge spume of fire. The wind buffeted these huge animated fireballs, and soon they were being blown onto the mainland of Canvey Island.

Looking anxiously from his office, Kevin Manwaring saw the sudden spurt of fiery activity. "Christ! What the hell's happening?" He shouted. He picked up the intercom phone and tried to contact Jim. There was no reply. Kevin looked nervously around, scrabbling for a desk phone and dialled the emergency services. But in the back of his mind, he knew that they could do little. His next thought was that at least he could save some of the other staff and himself. He rushed out of his office and down the stairs to the reception area.

"At least, Miranda was saved. Thank God, I sent her home early."

Bob was already at the reception desk. "Did you see the blast, Kevin, it's unbelievable." He looked very worried and frightened.

Kevin didn't answer but rushed to a microphone on the side of the reception desk. He clicked on the public address system and began to shout, "All personnel! Calling all personnel! Clear the building immediately. We have a serious emergency. Your lives are in…"

Before he could utter the word 'danger', a huge wall of flame burst through the windows and engulfed him and Bob in a ball of flame. Soon the whole building was a bonfire fuelled by the bursting oil tanks on the shore.

The shocked residents of Canvey Island saw the burning refinery lighting up the night in a yellow and orange glow. The storm continued to rage and now not only fire but flooding began to take place as the storm waters surged inland breaking the flood defences. The 'Ocean Queen' was now fully alight and being moved violently by the stormy seas. She was a big ship but the sea was too powerful to let her resist. The hausers began to strain and eventually red hot from the raging fire a cable snapped.

The huge ship began to move away from the docking area but was still held by two hausers. It would only be a matter of time before these too would snap and release the flaming vessel to drift down the Thames. It was like a fire ship sent to overwhelm an enemy. The hausers strained and were twisted by the sea but they quickly broke. The ship was free! Free to do its worst. It lurched away into the driving wind heading towards the capital.

The Oikos Oil Refinery was now a blazing inferno which was spreading to the rest of Canvey Island along with the floods.

The tanker large though it was had no one to control it. The crew were dead or injured and those that survived could not reach the bridge where the ability to steer and direct it lay. It moved out into the Thames estuary and by sheer chance was not grounded in the shallows but moved to the middle and began to run parallel to the shoreline. Soon it would reach the bend in the river at Stanford le Hope where it could collide with the river banks.

The sea around it was now a blazing inferno with oil spilling onto the raging waters. If it were to hit the shore near any buildings, they would soon be alight too.

By some miracle, the 'Ocean Queen' managed to navigate the river bend but was now heading towards Tilbury, Gravesend and Grays—all potential conflagration areas which could put buildings and people in danger. The wind continued to blow hard at well over 100 mph. The ship lurched towards Gravesend but the combination of topography and storm-force weather forced it away towards Tilbury and the docks. This could be a disaster of the greatest magnitude.

Bill Barrington looked out at the wild night from his office at Tilbury Docks and suddenly exclaimed, "Bloody hell."

He saw the 'Ocean Queen' reeling in the stormy seas and she was heading straight for the dock area like a massive blazing torch. Bill was stunned.

A number of people had gathered on the dockside watching the blazing ship heading towards them. Suddenly a uniformed security guard rushed out of a nearby building yelling. "Get back everyone. Get back now." Some began to retreat from the dock but others stood transfixed, mesmerised by the approaching floating inferno. "Get back." The guard continued to yell, this time through a bullhorn.

On the docks were piles of inflammable material waiting to be shipped abroad or driven to UK destinations. Bill was all too aware of what this would mean if the ship collided with the dock. He grabbed the PA system microphone. "All personnel to evacuate the dock front area immediately. You are in grave danger. Evacuate now!"

He repeated this message several times. Even the doziest person on the dock began to absorb the message and turned slowly, then increased speed in their hurry to escape the coming disaster.

The churning waters seemed to be on fire as spilling oil still gushing out of the tanker ignited. Soon the fiery river reached the dockside and flames began licking at the dock edges hurled up by the heavy blustery winds. The ship was not far behind and loomed over the dockside. Almost immediately the woodpiles were alight. People with hoses emerged from dockside buildings and began to spray water on the conflagration in the vain hope of dousing it. Bill now on the dockside himself could see what a hopeless situation it was and their only hope was to prevent its spread to the containers and main storage areas.

The ship crashed into the side of the docks with a huge groaning sound which was soon lost in the wild winds.

Bill felt hopeless and helpless but he knew he had to try to save the situation impossible as that might seem. His first thought was to remove as many containers as possible from the dockside but some seemed almost ready to burst open from the growing heat.

His deputy Neil Harvey ran to his side and shouted trying to make himself heard above the howling wind. "The problem is, Bill, those containers have either timber or bamboo flooring and probably…"

Bill finished his sentence, "Highly inflammable contents like paper and plastics. Yeah, I know. Ideal bonfire material!"

Already the flames from the water were licking at the stacks of containers and fires were beginning to catch on the docks. "We must try to get out the firefighting equipment and inform the firefighting service."

"I've already phoned emergency services. They're on their way," Neil shouted back.

"Good, man. Come on," said Bill turning hurriedly towards a large building on the dockside. He shouted to some men nearby. "You guys help us." Several followed Bill and Neil into the building where some hoses hung in coils from the wall.

They hurriedly began to unwind the hoses. "Turn on those taps over there," Bill wildly pointed towards two red wheels which two men began to turn. The hoses jerked into life and with two men on each, they ran out of the building and began spraying the fires on the dock.

After five minutes, some fires had been extinguished but the containers were now clearly alight and beginning to blaze brightly as the wind caused drafts of air to fan the flames to greater heights. The men on the dock began to feel the increased heat and Bill realised that some of those containers could have chemicals or highly inflammable material which could put them in great danger. He began to shout to the men to move away from the dock front waving his arms frantically in the process. At that moment, there was a huge explosion. One of the containers had violently burst flinging out pieces of metal which began to rain down on the men whose screams of pain were lost in the howling wind.

Chapter 25
Dartford Crossing (2)

Eventually, the 'Ocean Queen' was wrenched away from Tilbury Docks by the strong winds of the storm which seemed to have lost none of its power. The flaming vessel drifted out into the middle of the wide Thames. It soon became grounded in a shallow and lay there swaying in the wind. It was now lighting up the sky like some doom-laden beacon. Burning oil continued to spill out of the listing vessel giving a carpet of fire from the middle of the river to the northern shoreline.

Although 12.5 kilometres eastward, the settlements between Tilbury and the Dartford Crossing were quickly affected by the burning waters. Stationary vessels became alight and some broke away from their moorings pushed by the high winds. A number of burning boats formed an incendiary small armada and began moving swiftly westwards heading towards the centre of London on the rising spring tide.

Small boats were quickly blown on land causing fires on the shoreline. Others moved unhindered on their doom-laden way.

At the Dartford Crossing, the Queen Elizabeth Bridge could withstand most things the weather could throw at it, but the vehicles now queuing on the dual carriageway were beginning to sway as the winds from the storm grew fiercer. A high-sided vehicle wobbled dangerously in the wind. The driver obviously terrified leapt from the vehicle. It was as well that he had as the vehicle fell on its side with the main body of the lorry blocking the road completely. Drivers looked on in horror as the man now trying to stand up in the intense gale was being swept to the edge of the bridge. The driver in the vehicle behind jumped from his cab and struggled towards the man in an attempt to save him, but the wind was too strong and while he grasped his arm, both were hurled over the side into the raging Thames.

Panic gripped other drivers who began to reach for their phones to contact the emergency services. They were now marooned on a high bridge in a howling storm. However, the emergency services themselves were unable to act in the intense winds and were blocked by more trucks heaving over to one side causing more obstruction and reducing any attempt of a rescue vehicle reaching them to nil.

Dartford Tunnel below was rapidly flooding. Traffic had been stopped from entering and a huge build-up of traffic began.

Mike Scher, the traffic officer, had ordered a closure barrier across the flooding tunnels. His second-in-command, PC Jean Fairclough, hurried over to Mike.

"It's up but some bloody nutter insisted on trying to get through at the last minute. I couldn't stop him."

"There's always idiots! He might make it through but I'm damn sure his vehicle won't." They resumed the task of stopping the oncoming traffic and turning it back. A lot of drivers were none too happy.

"I've got to get to the north side," one driver pleaded. "My son's birthday party starts in half an hour."

"I'm sorry, Sir. It's too dangerous. If I let you through, you may never see your son again and it would also give a bad example to all those others waiting," Jean spoke severely with a withering look on her face. The driver got to the point quickly and began turning his car around.

Meanwhile, Mike had pulled out a bullhorn from the back of his patrol car and began to address the tailback of vehicles. "The tunnels are closed. I repeat the tunnels are closed. Please turn around and try another route."

He repeated this several times but some drivers had not heard the message in the howling wind and began to get out of their cars. The rain pelted down soaking them.

Another police officer emerged from the left tunnel and addressed Mike. "There's quite a few vehicles stuck down there. We're trying to get the drivers out but both tunnels are filling up fast. We may be too late."

"Is there anything we can do?"

He looked grimly at Mike, "Those that are able to get out of their vehicles can try to escape along the side pedestrian walkways but given the rate the water is rising, it is touch and go and I'm pretty sure, some won't make it."

Water began to swirl around their boots and it was plain that it was rising fast and beginning to lap at the tyres of the vehicles which headed the stationary queue. Eventually, vehicles began trying to reverse or turn around. It was becoming chaotic with horns blowing and heads leaning out of windows shouting abuse.

At the Blue Water shopping mall, Jack Rollins unloaded his last batch of cartons and decided to take a break and have a cigarette in the cab. The Marks and Spencer storeman closed the loading bay doors at the back of the shop. "Jack," he shouted. "Be careful driving back across the Dartford Crossing, this storm looks pretty nasty,"

Jack waved and smiled to reassure the guy. He climbed into his cab and lit up. His parked van looked out over the Blue Water site and its triangular shape. A post with a welcome to Blue Water sign boasted that it had 330 stores, 40 cafes and restaurants and a 17-screen cinema plus various leisure outlets. He sat smoking contentedly with the increasingly strong wind pummelling the side of his van. After a few puffs, he leaned forward and noticed the water beginning to surround his vehicle. Blue Water was so near the Thames that it could be vulnerable to a large surge in flood waters. This was it.

Alarmed, Jack turned on his engine and began to move forward down a slope to get to the mall's exit. The bottom of the slope had filled with water and by this time had reached a meter in depth. Jack tried to rush his vehicle through the rising enormous puddle but the van stalled at the deepest point. He switched the engine on and off several times but with no result. The van was completely dead. Jack opened his cab door and looked down. The water was now lapping through the door and beginning to fill the vehicle. What should he do? Stay in the van or make a run for it.

He jumped out of the van and landed up to his waist in cold water. The wind nearly knocked him over. He waded to the edge of the ever-growing puddle with difficulty, eventually reaching a patch of dry land. He looked around and saw hundreds of people panicking as it seemed there was no way out of the mall. No buses seemed to be running although a number of people stood by rain-swept bus stops looking bedraggled and mournfully hoping one would turn up.

Jack realised that the only way out would be on foot and with the rising tide of water that was looking increasingly difficult. He knew Blue Water quite well and was aware that the bowl-shaped landscape of the mall could entrap people in such circumstances. He looked around and saw dozens of people making for the exits on foot. Mothers had babies in their arms having abandoned their buggies and prams. They had taut grim expressions on their faces as they gripped their howling infants in their arms. An elderly couple was trying valiantly to stay upright.

A man at a first-floor window of an office began shouting to people to come indoors out of the storm and the floods, but his words were mainly blown away in the wind. Some got the gist and were turning around and heading for the buildings and mall entranceways. Others tried to battle on towards the exits but were blown over and fell into the ever-enlarging puddles.

Chapter 26
Thames Barrier

Andy and Mark watched Fiona leave for the COBRA meeting and decided it was a waiting game. Their mobile phones kept them updated on the progress s of the storm as it made its chaotic way down the Thames. They kept asking for news from the Thames Barrier staff who were very much preoccupied by events. Eventually, after much pestering, Gareth Stevens finally emerged and let them stay by the barrier entrance which afforded them some protection from the weather.

"We shouldn't be letting you in here but your persistence seems to have paid off. What is it you want to know?"

Mark went straight for the questioning nagging at him since his return to the capital.

"Will the barrier be raised and given the strength of the storm will there be a possibility it will be breached?"

"We have now reached the conclusion that the barrier will have to be raised. The Met Office and the Environment Agency are positive that the storm will be powerful. Fifteen metres high waves have been reported at the mouth of the Thames and they seem to be getting worse. This obviously means that we are faced with an extreme weather situation. As to your second question, we cannot possibly know if the barrier will be breached and we are unlikely to give you a definite answer, partly because we don't know, and partly because we do not want to alarm the general public. If your paper reported that, there could be panic and that would be a very bad situation indeed."

"So when will the barrier be raised?" Mark asked impatiently.

"That is about to take place. We like to have the barrier in position long before the tidal rush reaches us. So if you'll excuse me, gentlemen, I have work to do." With that, he ushered the two men outside.

"I'll get some pix as the barrier rises," said Andy.

Just then Mark's mobile rang. It was Fiona. She sounded breathless.

"It looks bad. Possibly very bad!"

"What do you mean?" Mark demanded.

"This tidal wave coming up the Thames is not just the usual thing the barrier can deal with. It's been described as a Tsunami."

The wind was now blowing harder and Mark raised his voice. "A what? I didn't get that."

"A Tsunami. A bloody great wave. It'll probably go over the barrier and as for the rest of London…" She hesitated. "It'll be a disaster!"

"Fucking hell." That's all Mark could say.

"You be careful down there. Keep well out of its way. Do you hear me, Mark?"

"Yeah, we will." Out of the corner of his eye, he saw the huge steel round gates of the barrier moving upwards. He ended the call and turned to Andy.

"Do you see that?" He said pointing to the barrier.

Andy already had his camera raised and was taking pictures as if there was no tomorrow.

The nine beautiful elliptical-shaped piers of steel rose above the river and the two outside and smaller sector gates began to move as the circular drums that create the barrier began to rise from beneath the surface of the water.

Just then the door of the barrier control area opened and Derek Lassiter emerged. "Gareth, you are needed inside." He looked disparagingly at the Mark and Andy. "You can't stay there in this weather, you'd better come in," he said ushering the two men inside.

"My pictures," said Andy in alarm.

"You can get pictures from the inside," Gareth shouted.

"I'm staying out!" Andy said stubbornly. "I can only get what I need from outside."

"Have it your own way. Are you coming in?" He asked Mark.

Mark nodded. "I'll get some inside info," he shouted to Andy and disappeared into the barrier offices.

The rain and wind continued but Andy was oblivious. He was only interested in getting that amazing shot. Soaked and jubilant, he was in his element. He ran up some steps to a higher level so he could observe the barrier in its entirety from above. The wind was blowing harder there and he pulled his thick anorak around him tightly. It was an increasingly wild scene.

Inside Mark eagerly asked, "So what's happening now?"

"The Port of London Authority has to be informed that the barrier is closing and it will warn all shipping on or near the river to have to or at least be aware."

"How long will it take to close the barrier fully?"

"We can close an individual gate within 10 or 15 minutes but the whole closure takes up to one and a half hours. That's why we need early notice of a decision."

"Will it be effective against the tide surge coming down the river? It's said to be exceptionally high?"

"The barrier is as high as an eight-storey building so it would have to be some surge?"

"Yeah, people are talking about a mini-Tsunami," said Mark anxiously.

"Where did you hear that?"

"Well, it is general knowledge…or soon will be. One of our reporters got that unofficially from the COBRA meeting and they got it from the Met Office and its stations around the North Sea."

"I don't deny that's worrying," Gareth paused and bit his lip, hesitated and added, "you see, it's been raining hard for the past week and that means a lot of water will coming through the Teddington Lock upstream."

"Is that bad?"

"Could be very bad. You have all that water coming down from the home counties, Oxfordshire and Gloucestershire and it can be a torrent by the time it reaches the tide waters of the Thames. It often creates huge flooding in Teddington, Hammersmith and parts of West London near the river. And that's without this surge coming in from the east."

Marked frowned and the penny dropped.

"You mean if the surge meets the tidal flood from upstream…" he paused and let the information sink in.

"Yes," said Gareth. "Then that would make for a huge catastrophe."

"If it happened, where would it likely meet?"

"I don't think if…it's more like when! Probably the centre of the city around the Houses of Parliament."

"Oh my God!" it was dawning on Mark that this was going to be a disaster of great magnitude. His first thoughts were to get the story and pics back to the paper to tell his family to run anywhere safe.

Meanwhile, the barrier control rooms were buzzing as men and women stared intently at their computer screens. Some were monitoring incoming information and others were sending messages on weather developments to the Port of London Authority and other bodies as well as receiving them in return. Most were monitoring the closing of the barrier and looking at the images from the external cameras positioned to show the process slowly taking place.

Mark pulled out his mobile phone. "Is there somewhere I can make a private call?" He asked Gareth.

"There's a clothes cupboard over there. You could use that." Gareth turned back to his computer screen.

Mark squeezed into the cupboard and began phoning Julie. After several rings, Julie answered. "Mark here."

Julie's mood was reserved and she merely said, "Yes." There was no expression of affection. Just an indifference as though she were talking to a stranger.

"Julie, you must listen to me and do as I say."

"I've been doing that all my life," Julie answered witheringly.

"No, no it's not about me. It's about your safety and the kid's safety." There was silence at the end of the phone. Mark continued. "There's a massive storm coming down the east coast and it's entering the Thames. It's not an ordinary storm," Mark paused and took a breath. "It is a storm that could create a huge amount of flooding in London. People's lives will be at risk. Some people are talking about a Tsunami."

There was silence. "Our house may well be in the flood zone. You need to find somewhere away from the centre of London."

Julie ever the kind one said against her will, "And what about your mother?"

Mark paused he now felt conflicted. "I have to cover this story—err it's a big one. Could you check my mother, OK?"

Julie harrumphed and said reluctantly, "I'll see what I can do."

"Thanks, Julie. I'm so sorry about all this mess. I'll try to make it up to you." The phone went dead.

Mark looked out of the windows and noted the storm was increasing in intensity. *I'd better get Andy in here before he's blown away*, he thought.

Andy himself had come to the same conclusion and was making towards the barrier entrance.

Chapter 27
Westminster Underground Station

Denzell Jones was about to finish his supervisor's shift at Westminster tube station when his mobile rang.

"Denzell? Bill Patterson here from central admin. The government is warning all transport sectors of a possible flood heading up the Thames. We must ensure passenger safety. This means closing the station with effect from now on. Lock all entry and exit gates."

"That's gonna cause a bit of chaos. What do we do if people don't obey?"

"Call the transport police and other staff. We can't have people caught in the underground system and drowning. Stick a notice up handwritten if necessary closing the station. We don't have a lot of time."

"OK, Bill, I'll do my best."

"Good. We are warning all stations in London whether near the Thames or not."

Denzell walked quickly to his small office and made an announcement over the public address system.

"Calling all staff this is code 'Inspector Sands'. Could all passengers be cleared from the station? That is the platforms, corridors, concourses and all other places immediately."

Directly after the announcement, Bill's mobile began to ring. "Denzell, it is Naseem. What's going on? Is there a fire?"

"No, Naseem. 'Inspector Sands' is code for fire but it's the nearest I've got for the oncoming flood."

"The oncoming…what?"

"This storm is causing a huge wave to come down the Thames and we're right in line. We need to evacuate the station immediately. It will almost certainly be flooded and we don't want any floating corpses so get on the case pronto."

Very soon other transport staff were gathering at Denzell's little office. Denzell pointed at one of his staff.

"Jack, come here." Denzell opened a metal cupboard and after a few seconds of searching came out with six laminated notices which stated 'This station is now closed until further notice'. He handed them to Jack. "I want you to hang these on all entrances and exits as quickly as you can. Can you help him? There's also three A boards so you can Sellotape them on that as well." Naseem nodded and took three of the notices from Jack. Denzell waved them both to the back of the office where the A boards were stacked.

"The rest of you get passengers out of the station right now." Denzell waved his arm for them to go.

He then picked up the microphone for the public address system. He clicked it on. "Ladies and gentlemen, this is an official public announcement, can you please leave the station immediately? This station is now closed. No more trains will be running until further notice. I repeat please leave the station immediately."

Denzell then found the loop tape with an official evacuation request and put it on permanent play. These had been put in all stations since the terrorist bombings began. He then searched in the metal cupboard and pulled out a bull horn and rushed out to see if the orders were being followed. As he walked rapidly up the corridor, a booming voice began to broadcast. "This is an official announcement. All passengers must evacuate the station immediately. Proceed calmly and quickly to the nearest exit. This is an official announcement. All passengers must evacuate the station immediately. Proceed calmly and quickly to the nearest exit."

As he moved hurriedly between the confused passengers, Denzell switched on his bullhorn and urged people to evacuate. A middle-aged burly man grabbed him by the arm. "Hey, what's happening, mate? I've got to get to Waterloo in ten minutes." Denzell snatched his arm away.

"There are no trains. You won't be able to make that journey. Leave the station as fast as you can...now!" Denzell growled at the man and hurried on. The man both puzzled and annoyed turned slowly and began to make his way towards the exit. Very soon, crowds began to surge through the station system. Despite the appeals to remain calm, people began hurling themselves at the escalators and bigger men began thrusting people aside to ascend the moving stairs. Scuffles broke out with some shouting but most people remained composed.

Denzell helped a woman with a twin buggy up the stairs to the foot of the escalator. He then stood and urged the perplexed-looking droves of people to make their way out of the station as quickly as possible. After about five minutes, the surge of people lessened and the station was virtually empty all but for a few stragglers.

Then he began to hear the rumble.

Chapter 28
Belmarsh Prison (2)

High winds swirled around the groups of prisoners waiting to be moved out. Already flood water was beginning to cover the recreation areas.

"Hurry up, it is bloody wet and freezing out here," yelled a prisoner.

"Alright, alright, the buses are coming now."

"Where we going then, guv?" Another prisoner shouted.

"You'll see."

Just then, several buses hoved into view at the main entrance gates and came to a halt by a line of prisoners.

Above them, a large helicopter battled against an increasingly heavy wind. It swayed in the air and descended onto a wide patch of ground which too was beginning to flood. One of the prison officers in charge of the high-security inmates said to his fellow PO, "This looks very dodgy to me. I don't like it one bit."

His colleague bit his lip. "Well, we've had our orders, Bill. There's nothing we can do."

Eventually, the helicopter managed a landing and the top-security category prisoners were filed on board. There were 30 prisoners of various nationalities secured by handcuffs. As the first ones clambered aboard, the line shuffled along towards the boarding entrance. Some prisoners had difficulty heaving themselves up to the hatchway impeded by the wind.

Finally, the last man, a PO, hauled himself on board and the hatch was closed. The helicopter rose unsteadily swaying from side to side. On the ground, Brian Marshall looked anxiously at the rocking chopper. He turned to Governor Lee, "I don't like the look of that, Sir."

Governor Rosslyn Lee said nothing but watched grimly as the flimsy looking aircraft tried to battle the wind. Eventually, it moved north struggling to traverse the River Thames. On board, the prisoners and prison staff looked nervously out of the windows while the helicopter crew wrestled with the controls.

On the Dartford Bridge, away to the east, truck drivers saw the chopper dangerously swirling in the sky. They stared in grim fascination aware of the ominous situation. The chopper began to whirl in circles and it seemed to those on the ground that not only was there a battle outside against the elements but also inside as the pilot struggled to control the increasingly erratic behaviour of the machine. Suddenly there was a huge explosion and the helicopter dropped flaming into the river below. The onlookers were transfixed by the rapidly unfolding catastrophe. Pieces of helicopter debris began to flutter wildly to the ground driven by strong winds. The shell of the main body dropped like a fireball into the angry waters below.

Governor Lee held a mobile phone to his ear. He turned to Brian Marshall with a grim look and a grey face. "It's exploded over the Thames. They didn't stand a chance."

Marshall looked up and Governor Lee nodded. He turned away his attention now caught by the noise among the remaining prisoners waiting to board the last buses. There was much shouting and agitation.

"Fucking hell, guv. Did you see that?" A prisoner cried.

"Just get on board the buses. Double-quick," Brian Marshall shouted down the line of men. The few POs tried to cajole the prisoners aboard but there was a general air of reluctance and alarm among the cons.

Some of the inmates began to break from the line and make for the still-open prison gates. Some POs tried to follow them but were too slow. The escaped convicts soon vanished out of the prison onto Western Way.

Governor Lee immediately dialled 999 and informed the police of the situation, but it seemed that the police had their hands full dealing with weather-related emergency calls in abundance.

Chapter 29
News Flash

Fiona checked her phone for news on her way to Cobra. The BBC page had horrific headlines concerning the Oikos Oil Refinery fire and its spread eastward along the Thames and now to make matters worse, Tilbury Docks was alight.

She switched to an actual bulletin with movie footage. A BBC reporter stood against a backcloth of flames and smoke.

This is unprecedented. Not even the floods of 1923 and 1954 caused as much damage and devastation to Canvey Island. And now it is moving along the Thames with fires from a large oil tanker. Tilbury Docks has also been set ablaze and flammable products on its quayside are creating huge out-of-control fires.

Fire Rescue crews are braving the inferno. But all emergency services, fire rescue, police and ambulance staff are either fully occupied or on standby in other red alert areas.

We have just heard that Belmarsh Prison staff and inmates have been involved in a horrendous helicopter crash over the Thames. All crew and passengers are believed to have perished. Search and rescue teams are hampered by the extreme weather conditions and turbulent stormy waters whipped up by the moving storm.

Fiona switched off the phone and called the *Guardian* editorial office. She was put through to Julia Devine the editor. "Have heard the reports? This Storm Betsy is causing havoc. I'm just going into a Cobra meeting to get a government briefing but I think this situation is moving at a pace that even the government cannot follow let alone control."

"OK," said Devine, "get a full Cobra Report and send it in as quick as you can. Where's Mark?"

"He's down at the Thames Barrier. If that goes, that's big news. The whole of Central London will be threatened by flooding and a lot else besides. He has Andy Carpenter with him and he's set to photograph the whole thing. It'll be a great, if tragic story."

"Yeah, good, can you get Mark to send in reports pronto and anything Andy gets? Video stuff can go on the website."

"We could sell that stuff on too."

"Yeah, but get the reports to us now. That's the priority."

"Wilko," said Fiona self-consciously copying armed forces lingo.

She reached the Cobra building in Whitehall and showed her press pass to the security men who let her in. In a large room, a number of reporters were gathered and TV camera operators jostled each other for the best shots as did the photographers.

The Prime Minister Emma Cooper looked serious. She shuffled some papers and stepped up to a microphone.

"The situation is very grave. Storm Betsy is now dwindling but not enough to cease causing the death of a number of people and a huge amount of damage to property."

"How many people have died, Prime Minister?" A reporter shouted.

"At present, we cannot be precise but we are continuing to monitor the situation."

"Yes, but what are you doing about it?" Another voice yelled.

"We have put into operation a number of emergency plans created for such an event."

"What kind of plans, Prime Minister?" Fiona asked urgently.

"I'm coming to that if you'll just give me a chance...err," she looked down at her papers and then gathered herself together and looked straight at the cameras with resolve.

"The Environmental Agency together with the rescue services and government departments have implemented a three-point plan to evacuate those people nearest to the River Thames and in zones likely to flood. This is now taking place and we urge people to remain calm and proceed as the authorities have advised as quickly and as calmly as possible."

Another reporter pushed forward. "Prime Minister, I hear that the privatised agencies that the previous government gave many contracts to are now completely unable to cope with the situation. Is that true?"

Emma Cooper looked flustered. "Those companies working for the government will be fully backed up by the armed forces and other public sector agencies. We will work together."

Other reporters began shouting questions but the prime minister picked up her papers and said, "Now ladies and gentlemen, I have an important series of meetings. We will keep you fully informed." She then moved from the room amidst a cacophony of loud talking as reporters began sending in copies to their media outlets.

Fiona pushed through the mob and once outside she spotted James Turnbull her civil servant insider. "Hey, James," she shouted.

He turned and reluctantly faced her. "I haven't got much time."

"What's really going on?" She shoved her phone now on record mode under his nose.

James looked very annoyed. "This is strictly off the record and no sources quoted."

"OK. So what's really happening?"

"Everything you heard in there is true but, of course, it's not the whole picture. The emergency services are pushed to their limit and some can hardly cope. The private contractors don't really want to know and they don't have the resources. Most offered the government their cheapest bids when given contracts and they have proved inadequate even in 'normal' times, whatever that is."

"So you're saying that the overall government response is not up to the job?" Fiona said disbelievingly.

"That's about it. I'm as disgusted as you are. That's why I'm giving you this stuff."

"But what about the EA evacuation plans?"

"Just paper exercises. Nobody in any government and local government positions believe they will be effective. All you can say is that they might be better than nothing. This is already developing into a very chaotic and dangerous situation. Even Whitehall is under threat from flooding and there are plans to move number 10 personnel to another location."

"Do you mean the government is being evacuated?"

"Yup. Whitehall has flooded before but this time, it will be much, much worse. God knows what will happen to Parliament. It's actually on the bloody river. Sorry, Fiona, I have to go now." And with that, he rushed off after the prime minister's entourage.

Fiona stood a little stunned.

She walked to the nearest cafe and ordered a strong black coffee. She sat down, took out her laptop and began to file her report referring to James Turnbull as 'a reliable source'.

When she finished, she pulled out her mobile and rang Mark.

"What's going down at the barrier?"

"It's expected that the barrier may be breached. There are reports of a Tsunami coming down the Thames."

"A Tsunami? Where the hell did that come from?"

"Some climatologists the barrier people have been in contact with say that a small opening has occurred in the North Sea creating a Tsunami effect. It's very unusual but it has happened in the past. This will add height and power to your 'Bump', Fiona. If that happens it could be very bad."

"It's very bad already, Mark. Have you heard about Canvey Island and Tilbury Docks as well as Belmarsh Prison? It seems like chaos everywhere."

"I've had instructions from Julia Devine to file stories immediately."

Mark was stunned by the news of Canvey Island. It was like a curse on him.

"You still there, Mark?"

"Oh, yeah. I'll get on it."

"Good. I'll cover the official outlets such as the Met Office, Environmental Agency and emergency services. It could be a huge story if the Thames Barrier is breached by this Tsunami."

"Er...right," Mark managed to say and Fiona rang off.

Chapter 30
COBRA Three

Fiona sat with other media personnel waiting for another announcement from the prime minister in the Cabinet Briefing rooms at 70 Whitehall. While she waited, she caught up with breaking news on her iPhone tuning into the various news networks. Stories of tragedy and disaster were now the dominant news stories of the day. The storm and the waves it had caused were passing down the Thames creating chaos and mayhem.

Many riverside properties were now aflame and the burning river continued on its determined way to the end of destruction. Riverboats of all shapes and sizes had been smashed to pieces or set ablaze by the unrelenting surge tide as it sped westward. Some of this wreckage had been hurled onto the river banks or had been stuck on struts and stations protruding from bridges and other riverside structures.

People who had ignored government warnings to stay away from the river area had been injured or killed in trying to rescue their boats, possessions even their pets. Many lives had been lost and the emergency services were in total hyper drive trying to deal with an impossible situation.

Flooding was increasingly impeding traffic as river water spilled over the embankments and onto adjacent roads and walkways. Huge puddles had accumulated under bridges where a dip took the road a little deeper. Vehicles were abandoned as panic stricken drivers attempted to drive through the deepening expanses of water and got stuck in the process. This caused backups and traffic jams and soon these queues turned into grid locks.

Drivers began to abandon their cars and vehicles in an attempt to get home or just to safety. London was beginning to grind to a halt.

Emergency vehicles were now finding it impossible to get through. Ambulances and police cars were stuck. Helicopters could not be used because of the high winds caused by the storm.

Fiona looked up from her mobile in response to a number of people entering the room. The prime minister took her place at the podium flanked by a number of experts and officials. She coughed slightly into the microphone and made the following announcement.

"The storm situation has become increasingly worse but the emergency services are coping as best they can. All ambulance and fire and rescue services are on full alert. We are urging people not to panic and if they are in relatively high up buildings to stay there until the storm subsides. Workers in the centre of London or near the river are advised to move away from the river if they can do so or stay put in safe buildings. All train stations and other transport facilities are closed until further notice."

A reporter suddenly interrupted the speech, "Does this mean the emergency services are unable to cope, Prime Minister?"

Before she could answer, another journalist loudly interjected, "Are the Environment Agency Emergency plans not working then, Prime Minister?"

A slight expression of panic briefly flickered across Emma's face but she made an immediate recovery. "As I have said, we are doing everything in our power to alleviate the situation in this unprecedented event," she said forcefully.

"You say 'unprecedented', Prime Minister," Fiona swiftly intervened, "but climatologists and even the Environment Agency have been warning for years that such an event could happen and yet it seems the government attempts to deal with the situation have been somewhat limited, to say the least."

"All the resources of the state are being utilised to deal with the situation. Ladies and gentlemen, I must leave it there. We will keep you informed of events." With that, she turned and left the room with a number of reporters loudly demanding more information and answers.

Fiona made her way out to file her story and noticed James, her 'friendly' civil servant. He seemed somewhat reluctant to acknowledge her but Fiona confronted him. "What's the nitty gritty, James?"

He looked slightly flustered and said, "You'd better come outside. You go out first and I'll follow in five minutes."

"Are you sure?" Fiona seemed sceptical.

"I can't be seen to be speaking to the press. How about I meet you at the National Gallery cafe in 15 minutes?"

"OK. I'll be there."

Fiona walked out into the wild weather. The wind and rain lashed against her as she struggled along Whitehall. There was water beginning to cover the roads and she hurried as quickly as she could to Trafalgar Square and the National Gallery. She went into the main door but an official said, "I'm sorry, but due to the weather, we are closing now."

She turned round and stood on the steps outside. She took out her phone and called James.

"What's up, Fiona?"

"The National Gallery is closed."

"OK, we'll try St Martin's Church Crypt cafe. If that's closed, I'll meet you outside."

Fiona walked along the side of Trafalgar Square to St Martin's Church and much to her relief, she found it open. She descended the stairs into the cafeteria and lined up for a coffee, found an empty table near the entrance and waited. She sipped her coffee slowly and a few minutes later, she spotted James. She waved for him to come over.

"I'll get you a drink. Coffee?"

"Yeah, that would be very welcome," said James.

"Anything to eat?"

"No, coffee's fine."

Soon Fiona returned and placed the mug in front of him. He picked it up and drank rapidly. "I needed that. Something stronger would be even better though."

"What's happening or should I say not happening?"

James put down his mug looked around the room as if to gather strength and sighed.

"It's bloody chaos. There just too much going on. The emergency services resources are stretched to the limit. I'm afraid, it's already turning from a meteorological disaster into a governmental one. They just can't cope. The cutbacks over the years have taken their toll. Instead of upping the budgets for the environmental agency, the emergency services and all the other agencies needed to cope with this situation, there has been consistent cutting. Even when the budget stood still, it was undermined by inflation. It's now a series of skeleton services."

Fiona now had her mobile phone recorder on and her notebook out.

"You see," James continued, "there are no votes in flood control measures and all the rest as this would mean putting up taxes and that is a vote loser. A definite no-no! Politicians are only looking to the next election. Three to five years is as much as they plan ahead mostly. It's a mess."

"So what is the government actually doing?"

"They are doing their best with limited resources but now the armed forces have been called in. They're pulling out all the stops. I don't think it will be enough. It'll be a sticking plaster over a gaping wound."

"So what are the armed forces doing?"

"Mainly back up work to the NHS, policing, rescue work anything that is required."

"Is this being co-ordinated?"

"Well, they're doing their best but in reality, the left hand doesn't know what the right hand is doing."

"In what way exactly?"

James took another sip of his coffee and looked around the room as if pondering the question and preparing an answer.

"The Environmental Agency had made plans long ago with the emergency services and local government, you know the Mayor's Office and various local district and borough councils, but there were never any practice runs. It was all on paper. Putting it into operation on the ground is another kettle of fish. With that and cuts to emergency services, it is bound to be less than adequate. And that's an understatement."

James gulped the last of his coffee and rose. "I'm sorry, Fiona, I must be going. I'll try to keep you updated as best I can but I'm strictly anonymous. I have my job and family to think about."

"I understand, James, and thanks."

She then got out her laptop, wrote a piece and sent it off to her paper. Just then a voice shouted loudly, "Ladies and Gentlemen, we are about to close, could you please make your way to all exits as quickly as possible?"

Fiona packed up her things and made for the stairs but as she went up with the crowd, she noticed her feet were getting wet. She looked down and then up the stairs and saw the water was dripping down making little cascades. Water was seeping into the building. The floods were getting close.

Chapter 31
In the Lap of the Gods

Mark ended the call with Fiona and watched as Andy took photos of the turbulent Thames through the windows of the barrier building where they were now ensconced.

"I'd get better shots outside," Andy mumbled.

"That wouldn't be advisable," said Derek Lassiter over his shoulder as he looked intently at monitoring screens.

"What's the situation?" Mark asked. Lassiter seemed agitated and Gareth and the other barrier crew went about their work in silence.

Finally, Gareth said, "The barrier is now in place, but there are ominous signs that it may be breached."

"You mean it won't be able to protect London," Mark said incredulously.

"That's about it."

"The barrier's over 20 metres high," said Gareth. "Sixty-six feet in old money and you'd have thought that would hold most weather events. But there seems to be the coming together of elements to produce what's laughably called 'a perfect storm'. There's nothing perfect about it. It'll destroy a hell of a lot of property, disrupt shipping and sadly and predictably will kill a lot of people."

"God forbid," said Andy. "So what is this perfect storm?"

Lassiter suddenly took control of the conversation.

"You have this very unusual storm, Betsy. It hasn't degraded as much as storms in the past. Then there's the Spring Tide surge which will add to the bulge, and there's the so-called 'Tsunami effect'."

"Tsunami effect. How did that happen?" Andy said, now fascinated by the conversation going on around him as he clicked away on his camera.

"We have had reports that a fissure has opened in the North Sea. It's not great but enough to create added turbulence to the maelstrom already heading our way.

In short, it will raise the tidal waves height and that should certainly breach the barrier."

Gareth butted in, "And this combined with high river flows coming down the Thames Valley and hitting Teddington Weir could mean water levels could exceed nearly 4.9 metres in Central London. With that heading upstream from a westerly direction and the flood waters from an easterly direction, when they meet, you have the 'perfect' recipe for disaster."

Mark and Andy stood silent and stunned. Then Mark said, "It's climate change, isn't it?"

"We're not climatologists," Gareth said, "but the Thames barrier has had to be raised increasingly since it was built in 1982. In total, it has been raised over 200 times since then. But it's been raised over 133 times in the last 20 years, and 90 times in the last ten years. This would suggest increasingly demanding weather events."

"Fucking hell," Andy shouted glued to one of the east-facing windows. A huge wave about 30 feet high was heading straight down the Thames with what appeared to be flames spurting out of its surface.

"This is it!" yelled Gareth.

They all stood transfixed as the flaming wall hurtled towards them. Its height blotted out all light except for the flames as it crashed against the metal barrier walls. Water surged over the barrier and onto the surrounding land on either bank of the river. Flotsam and wrecked small boats were hurled along with it smashing into the barrier gates and then shooting over the barrier creating a maelstrom of swirling salvage-laden water. Then the mini-tsunami moved on westwards towards the centre of London.

Just then Mark's mobile rang. Stunned at first, he ignored it but its insistent ring caused him to turn his attention to it. He looked at the number; it was Julie.

He clicked on the call. "Julie, it's hell here. Are you OK?"

"I'm fine. But it's your mother."

"What about her?"

"She's gone missing again. I'm worried, Mark, with all this storm and flooding and she so near the river."

"Christ, she shouldn't go walk about now. Hammersmith is a well-known flood area. You don't think she…" His voice trailed off.

"That's the point, Mark. I don't have a clue where she is. Do you know where she might have gone?"

"Not really. I'll have to get over there."

"It's not going to be easy, Mark. Much of the London transport system has closed down."

"I'll do my best. I'll be there." He hesitated before ending the call. "I love you, Julie."

The phone went dead.

Mark looked drawn and grey. "What's happening, mate?" Andy said.

"My mother's gone missing. She lives in a bad flood area—Hammersmith. And not far from the river."

"Is there anything I can do?"

Mark stood silently and then became agitated.

"Yeah, there is. I'll have to file this story but that's gonna have to wait. My mother's now my first priority." He paused looking guilty. "Andy, do you think you could file my story with some of your work?"

"I'll try but I'm no words man."

"OK, forget that. A bad idea. I'll run now and on the way to my mother's, I'll send a story and copy you and Fiona in. If you could send your pics, that'd be great. Do you mind if I take the car?"

"No problem. As long as I've got my cameras and laptop, I'll be fine." Andy paused and said a little self-consciously, "I hope you find your mum safe and well."

Mark managed a weak smile. "So do I."

With that, he rushed out into the pouring rain and howling wind. The Thames was high and its banks were covered in water. The floods were rising fast. Mark ran up a slope to the car park, his shoes drenched with water. He found the car and opened the door but the wind wrenched it away from him. He got in the driver's seat and struggled to close the door. He started the car and pulled away passing through increasingly growing puddles. He drove down Eastmoor Street to Woolwich Road. Although traffic was thin, he could see ahead that it was slowing. He now had to drive from southeast London to west London. Although Hammersmith was only 15 miles away, it was a bad journey at the best of times.

He put on the car radio for any news and began thinking about a route to avoid the traffic and not get too near the river. He turned south towards Lewisham. By now, the traffic was moving at not much more than 20 mph. *Perhaps, I've got it wrong*, he thought. He turned off the main road and found a parking space on a side road to contemplate what to do next.

Just then a news bulletin came on the radio. "The stormy weather is causing havoc all over London, especially near the River Thames. Most river bridges are clogged with traffic. The police urge motorists and pedestrians to avoid trying to cross the Thames. Find another route even if it takes you a long way out of your usual journey." Mark turned the volume down and punched in alternative routes into his sat nav. He could see that going via South Lambeth and Wandsworth might be feasible. He figured that much of the traffic would be streaming out of London from north to south at his location. If he travelled from east to west, it might be OK.

"I've got to get this piece to the *Guardian* and quick," he remonstrated with himself. He pulled out his laptop and began writing in earnest. He described the situation at the Thames Barrier and the way it had been breached. He put in quotes from the barrier staff to beef it up. It was about 500 words long but he sent it to Alan Evans, Commissioning Editor for Science and the Environment and to Fiona McDonald. He also sent a separate copy to Andy, who was still at the barrier and asked him to add some photos to go with the piece.

He then phoned Julia. She took a while to answer. "Have you heard anything about my mother?"

"No news, I'm afraid, Mark."

"I'm now on my way to Hammersmith. It'll probably take some time. The traffic's gone crazy."

"I'm at your mother's place now, Mark. I've been asking the neighbours but they know nothing. I'll have to get back home now to deal with the kids." She hesitated. "Good luck. Love you."

Then the phone went silent. "I love you too," he said into a dead phone.

Chapter 32
Teddington Lock (2)

Julia rushed to her car talking into the phone. "You say the river is rising to dangerous levels and the build-up is backing up the river. Keep all gates closed I'll be there in ten minutes."

She leapt in the car and drove out of the school gates. She drove faster than normal but tried to keep within the legal limits. The rain battered against her windshield. Eventually, the car arrived at Teddington Lock where she hurriedly parked the car. She struggled to put on her heavy weather coat and swept the hood overhead.

The wind was now very strong and she struggled on the weir walkway to the Lock Keepers' Cabin. She flung open the door.

"Are we glad to see you?"

"Thanks, Jodie. It's pretty heavy out there. What the news up the river?"

"Molesley Lock has all its gates closed but they're not sure how long they can hold that. The rains from the past week are draining into the Thames at a fast rate."

"What about our gates?"

"All closed at the moment but we're not sure how long that will hold."

"What about upriver?"

"As I said, Molesley's hanging on but they've sent a warning. Further up river, are none too optimistic."

Just then the official lock phone rang and Julia picked up. "Teddington. Julia Standish."

"Oh, so you're back then, Julia, Sam from Molesley."

"Hi, Sam, what's the news?"

"It's pretty grim up here. This is a warning that we can't hold the river back any more, it's spilling over pretty fast. And that's the case right up the Thames.

All the other locks are reporting similar situations. There's a huge amount of water heading your way."

"Hang on." Julia held the phone to her chest and turned to Jodie. "How long can we hold on? There's a lot more water coming down the pipe."

"It's not good. The weir can't take much more."

"We'll just have to open some gates and try and lessen the impact on the tidal Thames."

She put the phone to her ear. "Sam, it's bad news. I don't think we can hang on much longer so we are opening some of the gates. We're going to try and drain some of the water off to lessen the impact."

"Well, good luck with that."

"We'll try to let you know what's happening but it looks like we're going to have our hands full for the next 24 hours or so." She rang off.

Julia looked out of the gatekeeper's house window upstream and saw a rising tide of water bobbing just below the top of the weir gates. Boats which had not had time to clear the weir were banging violently into each other straining on their hawsers and mooring ropes.

Julia turned to Jodie. "If those boats break free, there could be mayhem. I hope there aren't folk on board."

"No. We've checked most of them and they're empty."

"Let's hope so."

Just then a huge surge of water battered against the weir walkway splashing the lockkeeper's cottage windows.

"Here it comes," shouted Julia. "We better open the gates."

"Every other one. Nine gates in all. Then if that doesn't work, we'll just have to open all eighteen."

From their control desk, they pressed buttons and some of the gates began to open letting a torrent of river water career down into the tidal Thames.

A large cruiser broke its moorings and began heading towards the weir. It smashed against the heavy gates and was lifted up over the top crashing down into the river below.

"Open all the gates," Julia shouted.

As the sluice gates gradually opened, torrents of water of increasing strength, and as wide as the river surged into the waters below. Boats which had broken their moorings careered over the edge of the weir. Some turned on their side and others bobbed wildly out of control being pushed by the surge of water. This was followed by swathes of debris of tree branches, small bushes and broken boats which too swirled into the river below.

Julia and her crew watched in fearful fascination. In all her years on the Thames, she had never seen such a chaotic and frightening scene. The river hit the side of the gatekeeper's cottage and although up to the windows, the water did not enter the small building. Julia and her team gazed down the river to the tidal Thames. The height of the waters began to rise rapidly and soon seeped over the river banks and the towpath which was quickly covered in swirling dark brown water. Some pedestrians, who had not heeded the storm and flood warnings, leapt back to avoid the lapping waters and beat a hasty retreat to the roads adjacent to the river, but these were also beginning to flood.

Passing cars found it increasingly difficult to drive through the rising water, and as the depth of the flood increased, some vehicles were unable to make it through the deepening puddles. As one car stopped, those behind were forced to halt and soon horns began to blare along the flooded roads beside the river. People jumped from their vehicles and shouted at the stuck drivers. Others waded up to them and tried to help push the car to shallower water, but the task was becoming increasingly impossible as the waters rose. Marooned drivers began to abandon their vehicles adding to the already chaotic situation.

Back on the river, the waters from the upper reaches of the Thames poured into the tidal system. The surge at the eastern end of the river was now in a head-to-head collision with the torrent coming down the Thames Valley. When they met, no expert could tell what damage and mayhem would be caused. The situation was beyond an emergency but evolving into a catastrophe. London itself was at stake.

Chapter 33
Hammersmith

Mark eventually made it to Hammersmith. It had been a harrowing journey with traffic jams and people standing by stationary vehicles arguing who had priority at road junctions or altercations about people pushing in the long queues of traffic and similar incidents. Mark had driven south to avoid the outpouring of vehicles from the centre of London, but the journey had still been difficult. Eventually, recognisable roads appeared. He was in Hammersmith at last. It had taken over two and a half hours.

Soon, he was driving down the road where his mother, and now he, lived. He parked in the driveway and entered the house.

"Mother! Are you there?" He walked quickly down the corridor into the kitchen but it was empty. On the table was a half-drunk tea mug. He looked around for any clues as to why she had left. A note maybe. But there was nothing.

He rapidly looked into all the downstairs rooms. In the living room, the television was still on blaring loudly. He turned it off. On her armchair was a woollen cloth with some knitting needles sticking out, which indicated the beginnings of a scarf. On the table next to it, some magazines were strewn. It seemed she had left suddenly as if a thought had struck her and she was determined to go somewhere.

He ran up the stairs into her bedroom, half hoping she had gone to bed early. The bed was neatly made. She had not recently slept in it. He pulled out his mobile and phoned Julia.

Julia answered immediately.

"I'm here in Hammersmith but there's no sign of her."

"I'm so sorry, Mark," she said. "Have you tried ringing her friends and the support services?"

"Good idea, I'll do that now. Is everything OK with you and the kids?"

"Yeah. We're fine. We're coping."

Mark hesitated. He wanted to say 'I love you' but he just said, "OK. Good. I'll ring you back when I have some news."

He ended the call and ran downstairs to the hall and the landline phone which rested on a small table near the front door. Next to it was an address book. He began looking through it for names with Hammersmith area codes. He found a Jenny Cook and dialled the number. There was a long wait until the phone was picked up and a frail voice said, "Hello. Who is it?"

"Mark Rattigan, Rose's son. You haven't seen her today, have you?" There was a hint of hope and desperation in his voice. There was a long pause.

"Rose? Rose? Oh no, I haven't seen her for a while."

"Sorry to bother you, Mrs Cook. You don't know of any friends she might be with?"

There was another lengthy pause. Then her raspy voice came on line. "Have you tried The St Michaels' Community Centre? We sometimes go there."

"Thanks, Mrs Cook. I'll do that."

He put down the phone and flicked through the pages of the address book until he found the St Michaels Community Centre. The phone was picked up immediately. "St Michaels Community Centre. How can I help you?"

She's done the training course Mark thought but then quickly said. "My name's Mark Rattigan. My mother often comes to the centre have you seen her today at all?"

"Is that Rose you are referring to, Mr Rattigan?" Before Mark could answer she said, "No, she hasn't been in today."

"You see, she's gone missing. She's in the early stages of dementia."

"Oh, the poor thing and poor you." She paused briefly and said, "The best thing would be to call the police and report her missing."

"I think I'll do that."

"Best of luck, Mr Rattigan."

He phoned 999 and the phone was answered. "Which service?" A professional sounding voice said.

"I think police," Mark said uncertainly.

"What exactly is the problem, Sir?"

"My mother's gone missing. She has dementia and…" Before he could finish, the woman's voice said, "OK, I'll put you through."

There was a brief click and a male voice said, "Police, how can I help?"

Mark repeated his worries.

"OK, Sir, first, we'll need some details. Your mother's full name and address."

Mark gave the details. "Could you give a brief description of her and what might she have been wearing, Sir?" The police officer said.

Mark described his mother as best he could, gave her age and what she might be possibly wearing. He added, "She might also have on a light blue knee-length overcoat."

"And your contact details, Sir?"

Mark gave his contact details.

"As you may be aware, Sir, the emergency services are dealing with the storm and flooding and Hammersmith has been badly affected. We will do the best we can. The name and description of your mother will be sent to all officers in the vicinity. I also suggest you speak to the local hospitals. I'll put you through now."

With that, a ringtone began and a voice said, "Hammersmith Hospital. How can I help?"

Mark repeated his information prompted by the hospital receptionist. She said, "I'll check to see if she has been admitted."

There was a brief silence and the sound of a computer keyboard. "There's no one of that name been admitted within the last 24 hours, Sir."

"Thank you," Mark said limply. He put down the phone in exasperation.

I'll just have to look myself, he thought.

He picked up his mobile and began dialling the *Guardian* office. He explained the situation. Mark asked had Andy and Fiona filed stories.

"Yes, and good ones. Some great pix of the storm hitting the Thames Barrier. I was completely overwhelmed. It's absolute chaos out there at the moment."

"I'll do my best to do a story as soon as I have found my mother."

"I hope you find her soon, Mark."

Mark rushed out and knocked on the next-door neighbour's house.

The door was opened by a man in his late seventies. The man looked suspiciously at him.

"Hi, I'm Mark Rattigan. My mother Rose lives next door."

"Oh, Rose," the man looked relieved that he wasn't a chancer or worse.

"Yeah, she's got dementia and she's gone walkabout."

"I did see her go out earlier today. The weather's awful and I thought she's not properly dressed for it. No coat, hat, umbrella or anything…"

"Which way did she go?" Mark interrupted him.

The man pointed to Mark's left. "That way."

"Towards the river?"

"Yes, she could have been heading in that direction. But it is mayhem down there, haven't you heard the news?"

Mark hurriedly thanked him and made off in the direction the man had pointed. The wind buffeted him and the rain soaked him but he was in another state of mind to care. He eventually neared the River Thames. There was flooding everywhere on the streets. Mark began wading through the water which was now ankle-deep and covered his shoes. Eventually, he reached a T junction by the river where police and fire service personnel had erected a roadblock.

A policeman approached him and said. "You can't go any further. It's far too dangerous. You'll have to go back, Sir."

"I'm looking for my mother. She has dementia and she was last seen heading in this direction." He gave a brief description and the clothes she was wearing.

"I'm sorry, Sir, I can't help you, but there's an emergency centre set up in the next street. You might try it there. A number of people have been rescued from the river and the floods and taken there."

He nodded and turned round and retraced his footsteps swishing the water as he went. In those few minutes, it had already risen noticeably. He took the first turn on the right and walked to the next parallel road leading to the river. He looked right and left and noticed to his left a large number of people and vehicles gathered in front of a large gothic-style church with a high steeple. There was a slight incline leading down to the river. He walked in the opposite direction. As he walked up the road towards the church, the water became shallower with the rising incline.

As he approached, he could see that to one side, there was a more modern building, a large hall. In front, there was a sign which said St Peters Church.

Mark walked up to the church hall where paramedics were carrying people on stretchers and placing them in ambulances. Mark entered the main door where a man stood by a table with papers on it.

"Could you possibly help me?"

"I'll do my best." The man was wearing a St John's Ambulance Brigade uniform and a peaked cap with an insignia badge.

Mark repeated the story about his mother and gave him a detailed description. The man wrote all this down and then looked up.

"We have had a number of elderly people arrive but none answering to Rose or her description."

"Are you sure?" Mark said.

"We're pretty sure, Sir."

"Can I take a look inside?"

"Be my guest but try not to hinder the volunteer helpers."

"Thanks." Mark strode inside and into a large hall where rows of people lay on portable and makeshift beds. Others were on upright chairs with blankets around them. Some sipped hot tea and ate biscuits.

Mark approached a volunteer and asked if he could see if his mother was there. "Yes, of course," the woman said and asked Mark for a description.

"A lot of these people were caught in the storm. Had no idea of its dangers. The Thames can look so peaceful and placid on a bright summer's day," she paused, "but on a day like today, we are seeing the nastier side of being close to the river. There have been quite a few drownings. Swept away by the floods."

Mark stared at her in horror. She immediately said, "I didn't mean to alarm you. She's probably alright." Mark smiled slightly to indicate he did not take offence.

He wandered amongst the survivors. Some looked in a bad way. There was coughing and some were crying. It was a distressing scene. After five minutes, Mark walked back to the volunteer.

"I don't see her."

"Maybe she's alright and gone back home." She paused, "There's another centre like this further along the river."

"I'll try there." She gave him instructions as to its location and Mark grimly walked out into the wind and rain.

Chapter 34
St Thomas' Hospital (2)

James Thackray, senior registrar at St Thomas' Hospital, picked up the phone on the reception desk. He dialled 999 and a voice asked which service. "All of them!" he shouted. "This is St Thomas' Hospital. We are right on the Thames and we are being flooded and we need to evacuate as many patients as we can."

"I'll put you through to the Emergency Centre Thames Side."

"What's that?" James bellowed.

"It's just been set up by the Mayor of London to coordinate emergency services in London."

"Right, put them on."

There was a click on the line as he was connected.

"Thames Side Emergency Centre."

James repeated his hurried plea.

"Right Sir, you obviously get top priority. We'll be sending round some army personnel as soon as we can."

St Thomas' Hospital reception area was a hive of activity with nurses and orderlies pushing and manoeuvring wheelchair-bound patients. Others were carrying stretchers and struggling with wheelchairs down the hospital stairs. Now the electrics were out, the lifts had ceased to work. Once on the ground floor, they then had to attempt to negotiate the increasingly watery surface of the ground floor. Outside in the official vehicle, bays a number of ambulance crews were patiently waiting for their charges. As the first patients emerged from the doors of the main building, nurses struggled through the wind and rain. Ambulance staff rushed to help them and load them into the back of the vehicles. Shouting above the roar of the wind, an ambulance driver asked where they were to take the patients. A nurse with a clipboard whose pages were flapping in the wind and getting soggier by the minute bellowed 'St Georges'. They loaded the three patients in wheelchairs, closed the door of the ambulance and drove off through the driving rain. The next ambulance drove up to the main entrance and the whole line of vehicles followed parking behind in a line of ten.

Ten minutes later, several army vehicles appeared and men and women jumped out of the vehicles and waded through the now rising waters.

They entered the reception area of the hospital which was now covered in a shallow pool of filthy water from the river.

A youngish woman marched up to James at reception. "Captain Marchant. Are you in charge here, Sir?" She recognised the white coat indicating that James was a doctor.

"We have to get as many vulnerable patients evacuated as we can. We have started but run out of ambulances and places to take them."

"We'll do the best we can. Show me who needs moving."

"First and second floors, but the lifts out of order. The storm's taken out the electricity and we are trying to operate the emergency generators. So far no luck."

Captain Marchant waved her army personnel to follow James. Ten army medical orderlies with stretchers and other equipment climbed the stairs. When they reached the first floor, James walked along a lengthy corridor and entered a ward.

"We've evacuated the most mobile patients but the ones left need considerable help to be moved."

"Could some stay put?" Captain Marchant asked.

"Yes, if the floods don't go on too long and the aftermath is not so serious that it can be cleaned up in a few days. These patients need constant medical overseeing, supplies of medicines and feeding. If that can be done, then there would be no need to move them."

Captain Marchant surveyed the rows of beds inhabited by patients in various stages of consciousness. A man sitting upright in a bed close to them said, "What's going on?" Nurses and orderlies were quietly going about their business but silently acknowledged James and looked enquiringly at the army personnel assembling in the ward.

"It's OK, Joe. We're going to try to move you." Joe Bacon looked out of the windows that straddled the north-facing wall. Wind and rain hurled against the panes with water droplets running down in little streams. "It's bloody mayhem out there. I'm not going anywhere." Joe looked defiant and grimly stared in front of him.

James turned to Captain Marchant and said in a low voice, "He may be right. It might be better to leave patients here and do the best for them by bringing in requirements."

"What kind of things would you need, Sir?"

"No need to call me Sir. It's James. Well, we need heaters, food supplies and some portable generators that actually work. All our electric and emergency generators are on the third floor. We thought that would be enough to keep them safe and dry but for some reason, they have all packed up. We could also do with having our waste garbage removed. Not healthy for the hospital."

"Right, James, we'll do the best we can." Captain Marchant pulled out a mobile phone speed dialled a number. "Is that Sergeant Cook? Right. Do you have any portable heaters and stand-alone generators?" There was silence at the end of the line. Captain Marchant said to James, "He's just checking. While he's doing that, could any of these patients be moved?"

"Where would they go?"

"They could be transferred to hospitals on the edge of London." Just then she resumed her conversation on the phone. "Right." There was a pause. "Right. OK. How many? I see. While you're there, are there any hospitals with the capacity to take some severely ill patients? Right, phone me back when you know." She clicked off the phone and said to James, "They'll get back to me on bed availability in other hospitals but we can get some generators and heaters right away."

"Good. It's a start!"

Captain Marchant then consulted her soldiers. She identified a tall blond-haired squaddie standing at the back of a small group. "Perkins, come here a moment."

Perkins detached himself from the group as the others fell silent curious as to know what the Cap wanted him for. Perkins stood in front of Marchant and said, "How can I help you, ma'am?"

"You're a qualified sparks, right?" Perkins nodded his head. "Can you nip up to the third floor and have a look at the emergency generators and see what you can do to get them active again."

"Could I take Corporal Ghupta with me, ma'am? He knows a thing or two about electrics as well."

"OK, Perkins, but I may have to take him back if things get hairy around here."

"I'll need to get my tools, ma'am, they're back in the truck." The two soldiers left hurriedly splashing through the ground floor puddles. They quickly returned with a toolbox each in hand and took the stairs to the third floor. Passing hospital staff and patients rushing to and fro in a silent panic. They reached the third floor and turned to the left. A nurse was hurrying along the corridor looking at them querulously as they approached.

"Do you know where the backup generators are housed?" Sergeant Perkins asked.

The nurse seemed surprised and distracted by their presence and their question. "Eh?" She took a second or two as the question sank in. "Oh, the other way." She pointed back towards the direction they had come. "Right at the very end of the corridor, there's a large room. It's there." She then hurried past them and disappeared into a ward. The two soldiers hurried in the direction she had indicated and reached a large double door slightly ajar. They knocked and entered. A man in a brown coat turned. He looked surprised.

"We've come to help with the electrics, Sir. We're from The Engineering Corp. Middlesex Regiment. Part of the emergency team."

"Oh, right. The storm's crashed the main electric cables and we've tried to switch to these emergency generators but they seem to be kaput."

"Right, Sir. Show us where they are."

The man indicated several large machines and they walked over to investigate. The two soldiers examined the machines grunting to themselves as they examined the connections.

"They obviously haven't been used in a while and have not been properly maintained," said Corporal Ghupta.

"You're right, Sanjeev, these will need to be taken apart cleaned and put back together."

"How long will that take?" The man in the brown coat anxiously said.

"Don't know. Maybe half an hour, if we're lucky."

"If you need anything, I'll be in the wards down the corridor helping the nurses move things." The two men nodded their heads and turned to look intently at the dead machinery. Then set to work.

Chapter 35
Westminster Station 2

Denzell's mobile began ringing. It was his wife. "Are you OK, Denzell? Have you heard the news?"

"Yes, Doreen, the Thames is flooding. I'm OK but I've gotta go. I'm dealing with a situation now. I'll see you later." He switched off the phone before she could reply.

Just then Nazeem came around the corner. He shook his head. "It's bloody chaos. People pushing and shoving. They'd trample over their granny to get out first."

Denzell nodded. "Have you checked the corridors? Is there anyone left down here still?"

"As far as I know, only us."

"Well, do you hear that noise? That's water. A lot of water and it's coming this way. We'd better run."

They began hurrying towards the exit staircases. Then they heard the yelling.

"Do you hear that?" Nazeem said.

"A cry for help by the sound of it."

Meanwhile, the rumbling was getting louder.

"You go, Nazeem, I'll check platforms one and two. It seemed to be coming from that direction."

"I can't leave you, boss."

"Just go, Nazeem! That's an order!"

Nazeem reluctantly turned and began running up the now-still escalator.

Denzell hurried to the corridors that connected platforms one and two. He checked platform one but saw no one. Then he heard the cry for help again.

He turned and made for platform two. There was a couple with a baby buggy. The buggy had got stuck on the railway line. Inside it was a kid who seemed remarkably calm.

The man turned, "Help us, for God's sake, my kid's stuck on the track."

Denzell rushed over to the couple. The woman was very stressed and crying pitifully. Denzell gently pushed her to one side and grabbed the buggy; it was stuck under the rail somehow.

"We'll have to get the kid out and leave the buggy," Denzell said.

The man seemed dumbstruck so Denzell carefully lowered himself onto the track hoping the electricity had been turned off by now. Gingerly, but firmly, he leaned over the buggy and grabbed the baby.

Just then there was a loud roaring noise. "What the hell's that?" The woman screamed.

Denzell said nothing but handed the baby up to the couple. "Run now!" Denzell roared at them. "Run like crazy."

The couple took the baby, turned and began running towards the exit. Just as Denzell was climbing back onto the platform, a huge surge of water hurled towards him from the opposite tunnel. It covered the platform immediately. Denzell scrabbled to get onto the platform but the water was too strong. The tumult of water picked him up and took him along the line and into the tunnel.

Chapter 36
Westminster Doom

The wave surge coming from the east barrelled down the Thames towards the centre of the city and soon reached the Houses of Parliament. The waters from Hammersmith and the west met the eastern surge at this point. The river rose alarmingly by several metres. It had turned into a whirling mass of water which seemed as if it could deluge most low-lying buildings. The wind howled as rain slashed the Victorian Parliament edifice and most sensible people had long abandoned standing on the balustraded area which ran between the main building and the river. All except one—the honourable member for Maidenhead, Sir Claude Trentholme. He stood defiantly on the terrace like some modern version of King Canute commanding the water to recede. A policeman holding tightly onto his peaked cap struggled toward the lonely figure. "Sir Claude, I think you should come in, Sir," he shouted vainly to be heard above the sounds of swirling water and the shrieking wind. Either Trentholme didn't hear or he was ignoring him.

The water surges were becoming more violent and beginning to top the low walls of the Parliament building flooding the terrace area and running inland to find nooks and crannies it could squeeze through. Claude Trentholme did not seem to notice. He was deep in thought with a puzzled look on his face which seemed to say 'This can't be happening'. The violence of the storm increased as did the height of the wave surge which began smashing against the sides of the building. Chairs and tables on the terrace were shoved around by the swirling and rising water banging against the parapet and then back against the Parliament building walls. A chair lifted by the water crashed into Trentholme and he staggered to one side and then a wave suddenly hit him violently pushing him towards the parapet edge. He struggled to regain his balance but was hit by another surge which lifted him over the edge and swept him into the watery maelstrom.

Inside the building, parliamentary officials looked horrified as they witnessed the last moments of Sir Claude Trenholme. "My God, what was the man doing? It seemed like he wanted to commit suicide by an act of nature," said Jonathan Cook a young Labour MP turning in horror to Arnab Singh a fellow party MP.

"I didn't like him or his views but he didn't deserve that," said Singh.

"Do you think we ought to get out of here? Perhaps head home?"

"Maybe," said Singh, "but it may be difficult."

Just then, an official came up to them as the other alarmed MPs gathered in the tea room.

"Gentlemen and ladies, I think you ought to try to go home. The waters from the Thames are beginning to fill the streets of Westminster. If you don't leave now, you may well be stranded here." People looked at each other in alarm and began making for the door.

Outside, the waters were beginning to fill pavements and roads. People hurried along to the Westminster tube station but saw it was closed. Umbrellas were blown inside out and some sent whirling into the sky. People's faces were looking strained and some had expressions of panic. 'What shall we do?' They seemed to say. By now, Westminster Bridge was closed and droves of people were struggling north away from the river seeking non-flooded streets and relative safety.

Streams were running down Whitehall. Some civil servants who had seen previous floodings of the area stayed in their offices in the belief that the water would not rise above a certain level, and as soon as the storm was over, would drain away. The river overflow did not stop at previous levels but began to rise by half a metre and it seemed it was not going to stop there. Politicians, administrators and various officials stared out of their windows in disbelief. The water continued to rise and the muddy river was beginning to pour into streets off the main thoroughfares: Downing Street, King Charles Street and Great George Street surging towards Horse Guards Parade and St James Park.

Roads on the riverside were now well and truly flooded. The Victoria Embankment was now to all intents and purposes part of the River Thames with only Westminster Bridge above the water.

The only people who seemed to be on the streets were TV reporters, video camera operators and photographers. Several resilient reporters were battling the wind and rain trying to make a broadcast of the events unfolding around them.

One valiant woman struggling to keep her waterproof hat and hood on while holding a rain-sodden microphone was giving her account of events.

"The waters of the Thames have now risen so far that the lower levels of the House of Commons and official buildings in Whitehall and beyond are being consumed by the widening river. This is not helped by…"

Just then an inside-out umbrella flew past her head causing her to duck to avoid it. She valiantly resumed her strained report, "Not helped by the incessant rain that has fallen in the past two weeks. Many government officials like the politicians are deciding there is nothing more to do here. This is now a job for the emergency services. It is understood that the prime minister and the core COBRA staff are now meeting at a secret location away from Westminster."

The broadcast came to an abrupt end; camera crews hurriedly packed up their equipment and began wading in the rising waters to a place of safety.

Chapter 37
COBRA Four

"Moving the COBRA meeting place is a shrewd one, Prime Minister," said Anthony Hammond, the Cobra representative from the Environment Agency. "It wouldn't look good to be wading out of the Cabinet Office up to our knees in water. That would give a strong impression that we weren't in control."

Prime Minister Emma Cooper looked around at the pared-down COBRA meeting, her face drawn with weariness and apprehension.

"Well, how much control do we have over the situation, Anthony?"

"To be quiet, Frank, it doesn't look good. As predicted, there is a great deal of chaos out there."

"Can you give me a more detailed report?"

"The storm has caused destruction from the mouth of the Thames westward to the centre of London and beyond. As you are aware, the explosions and fires of the Oikos Oil facility on Canvey Island have virtually destroyed much of the surrounding area. People are being evacuated from their homes and the emergency services there are at full stretch. The only good news, if you can call it that, is loss of life was limited to those poor souls working at the facility."

"What else?"

"That explosion created havoc as the burning oil tanker drifted down the Thames causing a large number of fires on the shore and to moored boats. There were a considerable number of boats which broke their moorings and drifted down the river creating more fires as some hit other vessels and the shoreline. The loose flaming tanker itself created large conflagrations at Tilbury Docks and the sugar refinery at Silvertown. There are many buildings alight on the shoreline as we speak. The fire service is straining to deal with the situation. We are extremely short of resources." He paused.

"Anything else?"

"Perhaps the most alarming fact was that the Thames Barrier had been breached. It has been predicted for a long time that it was a possibility in particularly bad weather."

"What's the situation regarding Belmarsh Prison Joseph?" Emma interjected.

Chief Commissioner of Police Joseph Charles cleared his throat. He looked ashen and paused as if ashamed of what he was about to say.

"I have to be honest with you, Prime Minister, the picture is grim. We have recaptured most of the escapees but a substantial number remained at large."

"How many is a substantial number, Commissioner?"

"About twenty-five. The prison authorities are still checking."

"The helicopter accident was quite shocking," said Emma. "What about the prison itself, is it secured?"

"Yes, Prime Minister. The floods only affected the ground floor of the prison and the various wings have now been secured. It's now believed possible that some inmates could be returned to their cells. As you are aware, our forces are severely stretched and moving a large number of prisoners to other facilities has not been easy. In the chaos, you will not be surprised to hear that crime is on the increase according to our officers on the ground. Reports of looting of empty buildings near the Thames have been coming in as well assaults and robberies."

"Anything to add, Mayor?"

"The emergency services are at full stretch. The flooding is worse than anything we have previously experienced and this seems to be a disaster of record proportions. Areas underwater are increasing by the hour stretching back in some cases up to a mile on each side of the Thames. That's a lot of people to evacuate. On top of that, medical services cannot cope and the fire service is doing its best but they are dealing with both flooding and fires. Fires which in many cases can only be described as arson."

"What do you mean arson?" Emma said.

"There are always idiots who thrive on chaos and love to add to it. Robbers, pillagers, thieves whatever you call them will often fire a building to destroy evidence of themselves. Other fires begin when gas pipes burst and electricity cables snap."

"Anything to add, General Pomphrey?"

"I personally think that looters ought to be shot. That will send a strong message."

"We cannot transgress international law, General," Emma curtly responded.

162

The general harrumphed in response and continued, "As you are aware, Prime Minister, the armed forces are backing all the emergency services as best we can. We are ferrying the elderly and infirm to places of safety but are hampered by the appalling traffic chaos as people attempt to flee the city."

"What's the position regarding traffic, Commissioner Charles?"

"As to be expected—considerable gridlock on many roads. We've had to close all Thames Bridges except for emergency services. People are trying to reach their homes north of the river, south of the river as well as people attempting to flee the chaos in both directions. The police are attempting to bring order by closing roads and re-directing traffic. But it only needs one broken-down vehicle and the whole system seizes up. For example, many bridges have low underpasses which quickly fill with flood water and we know from previous floods, that if one vehicle gets stuck under these bridges then it effectively closes that road having a knock-on effect both behind and in front of the surrounding traffic."

"Another major problem, Prime Minister," interjected the mayor, "is the blackouts caused by breakages in power cables. As night comes on, many buildings without their own generators will be in darkness. Many streetlights will be out as well as traffic lights. Burst gas pipes are another problem with the potential to explode and add to the fires. We must not forget that water pipes will inevitably have leakages adding to the floods."

"I think I ought to mention, Prime Minister," Anthony Hammond interjected. "That this is just not a huge surge of water coming down the Thames from the east but also river flooding in the west. The rainwater running off the Thames Valley and further up the river is causing a huge rise in water. A number of weirs and locks have been overwhelmed by the sheer volume of water. The clash of these east-west running waters occurred around Westminster and that's the main cause of Whitehall being underwater. And why we are conducting our business here?"

"How do we move on from here?" said Emma.

"Try to organise rest areas and refuge zones in other places. Government services need to be transferred to other centres. Birmingham has facilities for administrative agencies, and there are many cities with places to set up temporary camps," Anthony Hammond replied.

"Haven't plans been created to deal with such situations? It doesn't look as though we have any plans at all. From what you tell me, it is pandemonium out there." Emma made the point, banging her pen on the table.

"Well, Prime Minister, the Environment Agency has long had plans for such an eventuality but over the years cuts combined with austerity measures have made those plans virtually unworkable."

"In what way 'unworkable'?" Emma glared at Hammond.

"We just don't have the labour to deal with the situation. There have been staff cuts in the fire service and rescue services generally. The NHS and other medical services have been struggling even in 'normal' times. That's the reality, Prime Minister."

"So what do you suggest, Anthony?"

"The armed forces have been drafted in," Major Pomphrey butted in, "but we have the same problem. Over the years, the decline in numbers in the armed forces has taken its toll. It's not just service personnel on the ground but the money and resources. We need more vehicles and specialist equipment for emergencies such as this. We can't cope with what we have at present and that's the reality of the situation."

"I have also had reports from London Underground and other railway operators, that there is much flooding in stations adjacent to the Thames," the mayor quickly added. "We have information that the situation is worsening and other stations are being affected. It seems the London Underground report of 2016 in which they estimated that 52 stations could be adversely affected by floods is coming painfully true. The underground system is closed as many stations near the Thames are flooded. This has had a knock-on effect throughout the whole system. Trains are unable to pass through the centre of the city and this inevitably means the whole system is paralysed. In addition, most mainline stations are closed and some badly flooded, for example, Charing Cross, Waterloo and even Kings Cross and St Pancras are experiencing acute paralysis due to the flooding."

"Well, what can we do about the situation now?" Emma said raising her voice for the first time.

"It seems obvious that we must keep the population calm and informed. This means giving regular news reports on what efforts we are making to solve the crisis. All media must be made available for the use of the government broadcasts—radio, television, websites and social media systems as well newspapers."

"It's essential that panic does not spread among the population. That can only increase the severity of the situation. Retaining control is essential," said Emma firmly. "Have we been in contact with the all TV and radio stations?"

"Indeed, we have. Their news programmes are eager for information and stories and inevitably they are asking what the government is doing about it."

Emma then turned to the cabinet communication officer. "Jane, what's happening in that area?"

Jane Novak had only been in post for two weeks and was still in essence finding her feet in the role. She coughed nervously. "We are keeping all media informed with hourly bulletins but we can't avoid revealing how dire the situation is for long. People know. They can see with their own eyes and are updated regularly by friends and acquaintances on social media."

"Can we slap a few D Notices on the media?"

"I'm afraid that would be like putting a sticking plaster on a gaping wound. I don't think that's going to have much effect now. Social media would inevitably bypass attempts at such restrictions anyway. However, we can control the official messages. That will have some impact."

"Well, try to keep bulletins and other communications as positive and upbeat as you can. We have to attempt to show a panicking public that there is some semblance of authority coming from the government."

Jane nodded.

Chapter 38
Newsflash 2

A BBC newsreader stares intently into the camera with a grim expression on her face.

"Here is a news flash. The present gales and river surges caused by Storm Betsy have already caused considerable damage to property and injury and death to people along the east coast of Scotland and England. The storm is now making its way down the River Thames. Fires on river vessels and shoreline buildings together with widespread flooding it is creating havoc. Emergency services are finding it difficult to cope. Firefighters are doing all they can to contain fires. Over to our correspondent on the ground George Buckley."

"Yes, Emily, I'm here at Silvertown near a huge fire, which can only be described as a raging inferno. It has overwhelmed warehouses containing thousands of tons of raw sugar. As our viewers can see, it is a blazing firestorm. I am here with Captain James O'Connor of the London Fire Service."

In the background, a red sky lit up the night as he turned and pointed his microphone at a harassed-looking man in a fire service uniform and helmet. There were black stains marking his face.

"Captain O'Connor, how are you coping?"

"I've been in the service for over 25 years and I have never seen anything like it. We are trying our best to contain the fire but it is so huge it seems like a hopeless task."

"Why can't the fire be contained, Captain O'Connor?"

"It's not just one fire but several each causing other fires as they spread. We are using our fire service personnel and equipment to the utmost but at present it may be that the situation will have to burn itself out. All we can do at present is contain the spread as much as we can."

"Would you say the government has not given you enough resources and money to do the job properly?"

"It's not my job to comment on such questions. You must ask my senior officers that. All I can say is that our present resource situation cannot cope with a fire of this magnitude. We do need more crews and equipment."

"Thank you, Captain O'Connor." George Buckley turned to face the camera. In the background was a curtain of fire and smoke. "I have had reports that several people working for the sugar company have perished and at least ten people have been injured, some seriously with burns and being hit by falling objects. I return you to, Emily Shakeshaft, back in the studio."

"I spoke to Jane Novak a spokeswoman from No. 10 on how the government is coping with the present situation."

Emily turned to a large screen showing a rather reticent and tired-looking woman who peered anxiously at her interlocutor.

"Jane Novak, what has the government to say concerning the situation?"

"The prime minister and the COBRA team are preparing a special statement very soon. The government is working very hard to deal with the emergency situation. You must understand that this is unprecedented. This is quite outside the normal weather conditions we expect to see in this country or indeed this part of the world. These conditions can only be described as 'freakish'."

"And yet climate scientists have been warning of such a possibility for years. Certainly over the last decade."

"Climate change obviously has played a role in creating this freak storm and the other weather events, but it was thought that such a serious occurrence would not come so soon. We have been working on climate change measures but they take time to bed in and obviously in this situation, we have run out of time."

"So really the government is, to all intents and purposes, ineffective in a situation such as this?"

"As I have already stated, we are doing the best we can."

"But couldn't you have done better had you taken climate change more seriously and put more national resources at the disposal of the emergency services?"

"We are calling this a number one emergency and there is an increase in money now going into the situation."

"Isn't that too little and too late?"

"As I say, there will be a special statement announced by the prime minister very soon."

"Thank you, Jane Novak. And now the weather."

Chapter 39
Hammersmith 2

Mark returned to his mother's house exhausted and depressed. He entered the empty and now cold damp building. The hallway was silent and vacant. He called out in desperation but no reply came. He went in the front room and phoned Julie.

"There's no news about Mother, Julie. I'm afraid I'm beginning to think the worst. I've been around all local emergency accommodations but so far no result."

"Maybe she's staying at a friend's house. It's early days yet. Perhaps the morning might bring some positive news. Do you need me to come over?"

"I would stay where you are where you and the kids are safe. The effects of the storm are still working through. I've been to the river and it is chaos down there. They've already pulled several bodies out of the water. The rescue services are unable to do much until the weather calms down. Everyone is struggling at the moment."

"Well, if there's anything I can do love, please let me know."

"Thanks. I…I…love you."

There was a pause and then Julie said, "I love you too."

"Gotta go." He ended the call and then dialled Fiona's mobile.

"Mark here. How's it going?"

"It's absolute mayhem out there though Andy got some great shots of the Thames Barrier being breached. Flaming waves towering over the flood barrier. Scary. Very scary."

"Are you filing to the newsroom?"

"Don't worry, we have plenty of material. They've assigned all available hands for the story. They're struggling to cope with all the material but a strong storyline is emerging. I think we are ahead of the game at the moment. What about your mother, Mark?"

"No news, I'm afraid. We're still looking."

"Well, don't return until you know she's safe. Everything is covered here."

"Thanks. You're a marvel."

She laughed quietly. "Just doing our job as you would. Don't worry about work, it's taken care of."

"Thanks, Fiona. Bye."

Mark put on the gas fire made himself a coffee and poured a brandy as a chaser. It gave him a degree of comfort but no peace of mind. He began to feel drowsy. The efforts of the day had drained him. He quickly downed the coffee and brandy and went to bed and fell asleep almost immediately.

Several hours later, he was awakened by the telephone ringing in the front room. He drowsily made his way downstairs. He lifted the receiver.

"This is the Metropolitan Police, Hammersmith Division. Are you related to Mrs Rosemary Rattigan?"

"Er, yes. I'm her son."

"I'm afraid I've got some bad news." He hesitated.

Mark knew what was coming. It was the moment he dreaded.

"I'm afraid your mother was pulled from the River Thames early this morning and was pronounced dead by medical staff present."

Mark's throat was dry so that he could hardly utter the words. "Where is she now?"

"She is currently at Hammersmith Hospital. I'm terribly sorry, Sir."

"Right…Oh yeah…Thanks."

"We would like you to visit Hammersmith Mortuary to make an identification if you could Sir?"

"I'll be down as soon as possible."

He put down the phone and sank into an armchair. After ten minutes, he phoned Julie.

"Oh no!" Julie cried on hearing the news. Her distress was palpable not only on Mark's behalf but because she had known and liked Rosemary. "She was a good woman, Mark, and she lived a good life with your dad. She was like a mother to me. I'll come to Hammersmith Hospital…"

Mark interrupted, "It's pointless, Julie, much as I appreciate your offer, you would be unable to cross from north to south London."

"Yeah, you are right, Mark but I feel so helpless…" Her words faded.

"You stay where you are and look after the kids until this is all over. That would be the best thing to do Julie. I love you."

"I'm so sorry, Mark."

"Don't be sorry. Be safe. Let's hope we can get together after all this mess."

"I'd like, that Mark. Love you."

"Love you too."

Mark put down the phone. He sat there for a while longer trying to process the situation. Eventually, he picked up his mobile and googled Hammersmith Hospital's telephone number. He explained why he was calling and the woman in reception said that he had to be accompanied by a police officer in cases of identification. She offered to contact them and call him back.

Half an hour later, his mobile rang and a voice said, "Detective Johnson from Hammersmith Constabulary here. I understand you want to make an identification?"

"Er, yes," said Mark.

"Can you be at Hammersmith Hospital reception in half an hour, Sir? I'll meet you there."

Half an hour later, Mark sat in a chair near reception looking at his watch and waiting for Detective Johnson. The hospital was like a madhouse with people rushing backwards and forwards trying to deal with the overwhelming number of casualties being brought in. Eventually, a tall man in a suit walked to the reception desk and the receptionist pointed at him.

The man walked across to Mark and offered his hand. "Detective Johnson."

"Mark Rattigan." They shook hands. "I've come to identify my mother."

They walked down the corridor to a lift which took them down to the basement. They were both silent as they walked along neon-lit corridors until they reached an entrance which simply said 'Mortuary'.

They pushed the door and stepped inside. Detective Johnson had obviously done this many times before as he turned a corner and approached a small office. A woman in a white coat looked up.

"Hello, Detective Johnson, I've been expecting you. Unfortunately, we're inundated with a much greater intake than we normally have."

Johnson nodded sympathetically.

They followed the woman into a cold large room with rows of grey metal doors. She approached one and said, "Mrs Rosemary Rattigan?"

Both Mark and the Detective nodded.

"I'm afraid she is not in a good state." She looked sympathetically at Mark.

She opened the door and slid out a long tray with a body covered entirely by a white sheet. She then pulled back the sheet to the corpse's waist. Mark forced himself to look.

His mother looked bloated with sagging cheeks and a drawn haggard face. He stared disbelievingly for several seconds before Detective Johnson said. "Is she your mother?"

Marked choked and eventually said, "Yes, that's my mother."

Chapter 40
Aftermath

By the second day, the storm had calmed. People were looking bewildered and confused but determined to carry on as normal. The emergency services tired but not defeated were doing their best to help those in need and attempting to deal with continuing emergencies of which there were many. The flood water while receding was still very much present. Roads close to the river were still impassable. The drains had been overwhelmed by the volume of water, and sewage and other waste flooded onto the surface. The authorities were now concerned about the outbreak of cholera, typhus and other waterborne diseases.

On roads further away from the river traffic, movement was only partially restored but abandoned vehicles still blocked many roads, and had to be removed and the water under bridges was still dangerously high. Some vehicles close to the river had been thrust into the water and had careered down the river until impeded by bridges and other structures. There they remained swaying in the river currents providing a strange surreal scene.

Barges, narrow boats, launches, sailboats, skiffs and rowing boats were similarly marooned. Some had been thrown onto the embankment shattering into pieces and sending floating debris down the swirling angry river. The wind while much less turbulent at the height of the storm was still strong enough to knock the unsteady off their feet.

Along the Thames, many buildings which had been set aflame had burnt to the ground and those that had survived were severely damaged some irreparably. Their smoking ruins testimony to an appalling calamity. The places where the fires had been particularly severe, such as Canvey Island, Tilbury Docks and Silver Town were in effect disaster areas with the surrounding population being moved to temporary centres to escape the flooding. The conflagrations had left virtually nothing that was recognisable. By the third day, after the fire, these areas were little more than smoking wastelands.

While Belmarsh Prison survived the catastrophe and was gradually getting back to some semblance of normality, some prison escapees were still at large. Those residents near the facility lived in fear and trepidation about the consequences of the storm but also the possibility of having a visit from a dangerous convict. At the Blue Water and Lakeside shopping malls, north and south of the Dartford Crossing, flooding had swamped much of their surrounding area damaging many shops and other commercial concerns. They would be closed for some time to come.

The Dartford Crossing Bridge and tunnels remained closed as did most other bridges across the Thames. London was now a divided city. The 200 bridges of the 215-mile stretch of the Thames were unusable or partially so at best. These included road traffic, railway and footbridges. Some were badly damaged and the smaller flimsier ones had been swept away or damaged beyond repair. This would mean no one could travel to work if their home was on the opposite side of the Thames. This was underscored by the closure of all underground and most overland rail services. It was reported that 35 tube stations were under water and a total of 51 stations were severely affected by the flood water. London was gridlocked in every way. A London Underground spokesperson said, "Anything with tunnels was vulnerable as water finds its lowest level and this is why stations which were not directly on the Thames, like Marble Arch, Seven Sisters, Stockwell and Finsbury Park were on the list of the ten most at risk stations and were accurately forecast as being badly affected by the flood waters."

Not only were all public transport services closed down but the infrastructure had sustained considerable damage. Electrical cables, power systems, damaged rail tracks, road surfaces, bridges and other structural necessities were no longer functional. London had come to a standstill.

More than 50,000 homes had been devastated by the flood and 500,000 were at risk affecting 1.25 million residents in the city plus tourists, visitors and commuters. Thousands more were suffering from power outages. Nearly 250,000 people were unaccounted for. Most commercial establishments and businesses were unable to operate. Shortages of essentials such as food, oil, gas, and even clean water were now widespread. There was the increasing problem of the hundreds of thousands of people made homeless. Evacuation centres were overwhelmed and thousands sought shelter and help with friends and relatives away from the centre of the city. Community volunteer groups valiantly stepped in to fill the huge gaps left by struggling government and national agencies, providing help for evacuation centres, helping clear and clean flooded homes and providing food and shelter.

Care homes had to be evacuated. Some staff fled leaving the residents to fend for themselves. Schools closed and some hospitals were evacuated or partially evacuated.

An air exclusion zone over London was put into force and as a result of this and the storm, many flights were cancelled or diverted. This caused chaos at airports in Britain and Europe. The public was told not to undertake non-essential travel.

Looting had taken place over a widespread area and the authorities had warned that perpetrators would be severely punished. Robberies and physical attacks on people were common. In some areas, law and order had yet to be restored.

People on houseboats, vagrants sleeping under arches and many miscellaneous groups of people had died in the deluge and many were unaccounted for.

Galleries and Museums flooded most notably the Tate Modern and Tate Britain. Even the National Gallery in Trafalgar Square had water seeping under its doors. The South Bank containing the National Theatre was flooded and all shows were cancelled. The Dome was completely flooded and much damage had been done to its equipment and the structure itself.

There was a drop in the value of the pound on the currency market followed by a drop in many stock prices. The London Stock Exchange was closed adding economic fuel to the conflagration. Social media and mobile phone networks were closed down for many hours as a result of the flooding.

The prime minister speaking from an emergency HQ on the edge of London made a broadcast to the nation:

"We did not listen. We did not listen to those who warned that this catastrophe might happen: climate scientists, meteorologists and other experts. Warnings were coming from other countries which had abnormal heatwaves, droughts and flooding with more severe storms; refugees fleeing these conditions which had reduced their lives to poverty and threatened their very existence. We listened to the climate sceptics for too long. We listened to the oil and gas industries for too long. We believed in their greenwashing. We believed we

175

could wait for technology to come to our aid and solve all our problems. It did not. The planet is getting hotter and this is what caused this appalling flood. We finally paid the price. We must learn—and act fast. Very fast, or the lives we have known will change alarmingly and at an increasing rate. What can we do?"